THE HAUNT. ɔECRET

A LIN COFFIN COZY MYSTERY BOOK 15

J. A. WHITING

J. A. WHITING BOOKS

To hear about new books and book sales, please sign up for my mailing list at:
www.jawhiting.com

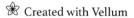 Created with Vellum

For my family with love

1

Lin Coffin and her husband Jeff walked along the brick sidewalks of Nantucket town with their little, brown, mixed-breed dog Nicky trotting ahead of them.

"So tell me again what's going on in this house." Lin had been born on the island, but had been raised in Cambridge, Massachusetts by her grandfather after her parents' untimely deaths.

Jeff ran his hand through his hair. He and his friend Kurt owned a construction and antique house restoration business and he was eager to show his wife the house they'd been contracted to work on. "A bunch of stuff. Some I've experienced, some Kurt has seen and heard. The owners purchased the house about two months ago. The couple doesn't live in it yet. They're waiting until the renovation and restoration are finished."

"Have the new home owners experienced the unusual activity?" Lin questioned as she pulled her long brown hair up into a ponytail. Not waiting for her husband to reply, she said, "It sure is hot and humid today."

"The homeowners have been at the house when some odd things have happened. Before we accepted the contract to renovate the place, they told us that the house might be haunted and they wanted to know if we could work in a house that contained a disgruntled spirit."

The little hairs on Lin's arms stood up. "Disgruntled? You didn't tell me the ghost was disgruntled. The owners aren't bothered by what's going on?"

"Sure, they are, but it seems they had a ghost in the place they previously owned on-island that they recently sold. The problem is their previous ghost was friendly. They've never experienced an angry one."

"You didn't tell me the ghost was unhappy. What makes everyone so sure it's disgruntled? This is an important piece of information. Why didn't you tell me?"

Jeff shoved his hands in his pockets. "Well, to answer your first question, sometimes things get thrown across the room."

Lin's eyes went wide. "Do people get the impression the ghost is aiming for them? Or is it just trying to get people's attention?"

"I don't know. I haven't been there when anything goes flying. Kurt was in the room when a candlestick smashed into the wall. He isn't fully onboard with the ghost idea, but he's open to them since he's had some strange incidents over the years. And besides, it's Nantucket. Most everybody here has *heard* stories or *have* stories about spirits."

"Does Kurt know about me?" Lin asked cautiously.

"No, he doesn't. I've never mentioned it. I know you don't want to broadcast your skill to anyone."

The dog and the couple walked around the monument located at the top of Main Street and headed further along upper Main.

"We might have to tell him," Lin sighed. "And back to my earlier question, why didn't you tell me this spirit is angry?"

"I didn't think that detail would sit well with you. And anyway, I don't know if it really is an angry ghost. Maybe it's only trying to make contact with us.

I didn't want to color your impression. You're the expert. I wanted to hear what you thought without influencing you one way or the other."

"Okay. That makes sense. I don't have much experience with aggressive spirits. The ghosts I work with want my help. They're usually sad or in need of assistance. The idea of an angry or dangerous ghost puts me on edge."

"The last ghost you dealt with was kind of scary," Jeff pointed out.

"Just because of its shape and form. Well, at first, it *was* scary, but then I figured out what was going on." Lin absent-mindedly reached up and rubbed her horseshoe necklace between her thumb and index finger. The necklace was once owned by her ancestor, Emily Witchard Coffin, and was found in her cousin Viv's storage shed, hidden there hundreds of years ago by Emily's husband, Sebastian, an early settler of Nantucket.

There was a white-gold horseshoe in the middle of the pendant that tilted slightly to one side. The design of the horseshoe could be seen in the chimney bricks of several old houses on the island and was intended to ward off witches and evil spells.

Sebastian Coffin had the design constructed into

his own chimney, but his purpose was not to keep witches away. The symbol was placed there to draw people who had been accused of witchcraft to his home where he and his wife provided them a safe place to stay and helped them integrate into island life.

After passing several of the homes on upper Main Street, they stopped across from a large white Colonial house with black shutters and a central chimney that was set slightly back from the road. The house had been built in the early 1830s by George Bean, a descendant of one of the early families of Nantucket. Bean had the house built on land that had been in his family since the 1670s.

Nicky wagged his tail and let out a sharp woof.

"It's a beautiful house." Lin admired the seemingly well-kept home.

"It is, but the interior needs a lot of work. The former owners let things fall into a state of disrepair."

"It's too bad that happens to some of these antique homes, but thankfully, the new owners are taking it in hand. And can afford to restore it."

"It will be a good investment for them," Jeff pointed out.

Nicky looked up at Lin and Jeff, and whined.

"Hold on, Nick," Lin told the dog. "We'll go inside in a few minutes."

"Are you sensing anything?" Jeff asked.

"Only my own uneasiness," his wife admitted. Lin looked at the houses lining that section of the street. Some were brick in typical late-Federal style architecture, another was an example of early Greek Revival architecture. Many of the homes dated from the 1830s to the 1850s and more than a few of the families who had lived in the houses had made great fortunes from the international whaling industry.

"Can you tell me anything else about the ghost?" Lin kept her eyes pinned on the house letting her eyes wander over every inch of the place.

Jeff shrugged. "Not really. I know candlesticks get thrown around, some tools have gone missing, things get moved from room to room. Doors open that should have remained latched. Sounds come from the second floor."

Lin turned to face her husband. "Sounds? What kind of sounds?"

"Moaning, crying, footsteps, screams."

"Have you heard the sounds?"

"No. The only thing I've experienced is my tools getting moved. I put them down, come back a few minutes later, and they've been moved into another room. At first, I thought I was losing it, but Kurt told me it must be the ghost. He was kidding, but then I realized he must be right."

"Do you see anything when you're in the house? Recently, you've been able to notice some shimmering when a ghost is around."

"No shimmering. I don't see anything at all."

"Do you ever feel anything when you're inside? A wave of cold air? A displacement of the air around you?"

"No, but maybe I need to pay more attention."

Lin looked back to the house. "Is anyone inside right now? Is anyone working here today?"

"No one is scheduled to work here this afternoon. That's why I thought it would be best to come by now."

Lin nodded, took a long, deep breath, and squared her shoulders. "I'm ready. Let's go in."

At the front door, Jeff took the key out of his pocket and unlocked it. He swung it open and they entered the large foyer to see a beautiful carved wooden staircase leading up to the second floor.

Nicky put his nose to the floor and sniffed all around.

"What about the people who used to live here? Are they still on-island?"

"They passed away. It took a few years for the estate to be settled and the house put on the market."

"Too bad. I was hoping I could talk to them about the resident ghost. What about family members?" Lin followed Jeff as he took her on a tour of the first floor. A few pieces of furniture and some books had been left in some of the rooms.

"They didn't have any children. The new owners don't think there are any remaining relatives at all. They dealt with the attorney who was handling the sale. There's no one to inherit. All assets are going to charities or universities or cultural institutions."

"Maybe Anton knows something about this place," Lin mused. Anton Wilson was a dear friend of hers. The older man was an historian, author, and former professor, and he knew more about the history of the island of Nantucket than anyone else Lin knew.

"This is the room I was working in the other day when my tools got moved." Jeff walked into a sitting room with a large fireplace on one wall.

"Is this the room where the candlestick got thrown against the wall?"

Jeff smiled. "Which time?"

Suddenly, footsteps could be heard walking across the floor above them.

"Do you hear that?" Lin whispered.

Jeff's voice shook slightly as he took a step closer to his wife and took her hand in his. "I hear it, and it's taking all my strength and willpower not to run out the front door."

A low moan floated on the air.

Lin stared at the ceiling. "It sounds like a man ... a young man."

"Can we get out of here?" Jeff tugged on her hand. His face had gone pale.

Lin didn't respond, she just kept staring at the ceiling. "We're not here to hurt you. No one who comes into the house wants to do you harm. I'm Carolin Coffin," she said softly. "Everyone calls me Lin. I've been able to sense and see ghosts since I was a little girl. If you need something, I'll try to help you."

A wail of misery bounced off the walls and chilled Lin to the bone. She could feel the spirit's grief and suffering. Her eyes filled with tears.

"Lin," Jeff whispered. "Maybe we should get out of here."

Nicky stared up at the ceiling and let out a whine.

The crying stopped. The footsteps ceased.

"I'll come back again." Lin swallowed hard to clear her throat. "I'll help you, if I can. I promise. I'm here with you now. You aren't alone."

2

As soon as they entered the bookstore-café, Lin spotted her cousin Viv arranging some hard cover books on a round table. Nicky darted off in search of Viv's gray cat Queenie.

Viv was the same age as Lin, carried a few extra pounds, had chin-length light brown hair flecked with gold that was cut in layers around her face. Her perfect skin was complemented by rosy cheeks and a warm, lovely smile. Viv's popular bookstore-café, Viv's Victus, was always busy with customers browsing the book aisles or sitting at the café tables sipping beverages and eating pastries, soup, or sandwiches. The early morning was often the busiest as groups of friends met for coffee, and workers, locals, and tourists stopped in for a beverage and a bite to eat.

Viv spotted Lin and hurried over to her. "Did you go to the house Jeff has been renovating?"

"I was just there. He showed me around and told me about some of the things that have been going on in the house."

Viv eyed her cousin warily. "You look spooked. Are you okay?"

"I'm okay." Lin looked over her shoulders to see if anyone was near, then she kept her voice down to nearly a whisper. "I heard the ghost wailing. It was such an eerie sound, it made me shiver. It sounds like a young man. At least, that was my first impression. He sounds so full of grief and sadness and misery. It made me so sad to hear his cries."

A look of discomfort passed over Viv's face. "Oh, no."

Lin was about to go on with her tale, when Viv suggested, "Libby and Anton are sitting in the café. Let's go join them. Then you won't have to tell this story more than once."

The young women headed for the back of Viv's shop, walked over to the table where their friends were sitting, and took the empty seats.

Libby was a distant cousin of the women and she had powerful paranormal skills. When Lin returned to the island a few years ago and began to see ghosts again, Libby counseled the young woman and was instrumental in helping her understand her ability. A pretty older woman, no one really knew Libby's age and certainly would never ask. Slender with short, silver-white hair layered around her face, the woman had piercing blue eyes that seemed to bore right into you, discovering all your thoughts and secrets.

When the cousins sat down at the table, Anton Wilson looked up from his laptop and addressed Lin. "What's wrong with you? You look like you've seen a ghost."

Libby inspected the young woman's face. "Have you?"

Lin sighed. "I didn't see one. I heard one."

"Intriguing." Anton pushed his black-rimmed eyeglasses up his nose and leaned forward. "Where?" The man didn't have powers of his own, but he'd been friends with Libby for years and knew about, accepted, and appreciated her and Lin's special skills.

"At a house on upper Main Street. Jeff and Kurt have been contracted to renovate the place. Some odd things have been going on so Jeff took me over there."

"What sort of odd things?" Anton looked eager to know.

Lin explained what Jeff had told her. "We hadn't been inside for more than a few minutes when footsteps could be heard pacing around upstairs. Then the most mournful sound pierced the air. It made the little hairs on my arms stand up."

"The ghost must have been waiting for you," Libby speculated. "Is it a man or a woman?"

"A man. I think a young man."

Libby nodded. "The spirit was probably hoping you'd come to the house. He must have been throwing things across the room and moving objects the men had set down in order to get one of the renovators to bring you by."

"Really?" Viv screwed up her face. "If a spirit wants to make contact with Lin, why not just appear to her wherever she happens to be?"

"You know very well, Vivian," Libby spoke, "that some spirits are bound to a certain place and do not wander."

"But," Viv persisted, "if a ghost really wanted to get Lin to help them, why not let go of what they're tethered to and float around to find her?"

"Because they can't." Libby's voice was almost stern. She looked at Lin. "Do you know anything about this spirit?"

"No, but the house was recently sold and the new owners are having the place renovated and restored," Lin explained. "The owners claim to have had a ghost in the house they owned before this one. Their previous ghost was calm and friendly while this new one is said to be disgruntled."

Libby tapped her index finger against her chin. "Hmm. I think I know which house it is. The couple was older and passed away about two years ago."

"That's right. They didn't have any relatives so the estate was being handled by an attorney. It took two years to put the house on the market," Lin told them what she'd learned from Jeff. "Do you know any more about the house?"

"I don't." Libby shook her head. "I wasn't aware that a spirit resided there."

"Maybe people kept it hush hush," Anton ventured a guess. "A ghost in a house can affect it's value. Not everyone is open to having a resident spirit. A ghostly presence can negatively impact a home's value."

"That's what John says," Viv shared. Her

husband John was a successful island real estate agent and broker.

"Did you get a sense of what the ghost might want?" Libby inquired.

Lin shook her head. "No, no idea at all."

"It will reveal itself in time." Libby lifted her coffee mug to her lips and sipped. "You'll visit again?"

"I will, but it will have to be when the other workers aren't there."

"What about Jeff's partner Kurt?" Libby asked. "He doesn't know about your skills, am I correct?"

"He doesn't know I can see ghosts on a regular basis."

"Well, he might need to be brought into the loop. Do you feel you can trust him?"

"I think so."

Viv piped up. "Could Jeff hear the footsteps and the moans?"

Lin nodded.

"And the other workers have heard the ghost?" Viv asked.

Lin said, "Kurt has had tools moved around and was in the room when a candlestick flew across the space and smashed into a wall. But I don't think the other men have experienced anything overt, but I think a few of the workers have heard the footsteps upstairs."

Viv turned to Libby. "Why do ghosts let normal people see or hear them at times?"

"Well," Libby said, "for several reasons ... to frighten people away, to warn them about something, to have someone bring a person like Lin to a location so they can make contact. If a ghost needs something, it's important they make contact with someone with very strong skills. A normal person doesn't have the depth of knowledge that special interactions with ghosts require."

Lin groaned. "I never feel like I have any depth of knowledge."

"But you do, my dear. It's buried deep inside you."

Anton said, "You have never let a ghost down. Not once. Your knowledge bubbles up when it is needed and gives you the ability to understand what a spirit requires."

"I always feel like I'm going to fail the ghost," Lin sighed.

Libby patted the young woman's hand. "The day may come when you are unable to help a spirit. However, it won't be because you lack the skill to do so. It will be because the ghost is unable to manage its emotions and expectations."

Just then, Heather Jenness came around one the bookshelves, looked about the café, and when she spotted Lin, Viv, Anton, and Libby at a table, she hurried over.

"Can I join you?" Heather, was a smart, kind, athletic-looking woman in her fifties with shoulder-length, light brown hair. She'd been dating Lin's landscaping partner for a little over a year.

"Have a seat," Lin encouraged.

"Would you like something to drink?" Viv asked. "Tea, coffee?"

"Maybe in a few minutes."

When Lin looked at Heather, her brow wrinkled as a sense of unease ran through her body. "Is everything all right? Is Leonard okay?"

"Yes, yes. Leonard's fine. It isn't that." Heather ran her hand over her forehead.

"What is it then?" Lin asked gently.

"Lori, my niece, has a friend here on-island."

The people around the table knew Lori. She was an attorney who worked in Heather's law office and had moved to the island about a year and a half ago. Lin had introduced Lori to her husband.

Heather went on with her story. "I understand

that the young woman is an online influencer, whatever that really means. She also makes Nantucket baskets and has a business selling them. Anyway, Lori told me that her friend has been acting oddly recently. It seems she's been receiving what she feels are somewhat threatening messages."

"What sort of messages?" Lin asked.

"Lori isn't sure. She's never seen them and her friend doesn't want to share the content of the messages," Heather reported. "But Lori told me her friend has been nervous and agitated lately."

"How does she receive the messages?" Viv questioned.

"I don't know the answer to that either."

"Has she gone to the police?" Anton asked.

"She has, but the police say there isn't anything they can do unless things escalate."

"What's the friend's name?" Lin questioned.

"April Blake. I know her mother, Leah."

Libby cleared her throat. "Is there a possibility that the young woman is fabricating the situation in order to use the story on social media to bring attention to herself and grow her followers?"

Lin and Viv stared at the older woman, amazed that she knew what an influencer was.

"April isn't like that. She's an artist, a maker. The

whole influencer thing was unexpected and surprising," Heather explained. "It sort of took off organically."

An idea popped into Lin's head. "Did you come into the bookstore to look for us?"

"I did. I thought Viv would be here and could tell me where you were. I wanted to talk to both of you," Heather admitted.

"Why?"

"Leonard has told me how you and Viv help people and sometimes assist the police with things that happen on-island. I thought you might be able to help with this situation."

"I doubt we can figure out who the person is who's harassing April," Viv said.

Lin's skin felt prickly. "Is there something else going on?"

Heather swallowed and nodded. "April seems to be missing."

3

"Missing?" Lin's eyes narrowed.

"April hasn't been in contact with anyone for a couple of days," Heather reported.

Libby sat up straight. "Had she scheduled a trip? Did she have a reason to leave the island?"

With a shake of her head, Heather said, "No. April had no plans to take time off or visit the mainland. Both April's mother and Lori have called and texted her, but neither one has received a reply."

"Does April have a boyfriend?" Viv questioned.

"She dates, but doesn't have anyone special."

"Well, maybe she met someone and they went off together for a couple of days," Viv suggested.

"Her mother tells me that's out of character. She's never done that. April texts and talks with her mother multiple times a day. Leah is worried about her daughter."

"Did she go to the police? Did Leah report her concerns to the police?" Anton asked.

Heather nodded. "She called them this morning, but they said it isn't unusual for an adult to be out of contact for a few days. They asked her to call again in a couple of days if her daughter doesn't show up."

"That's frustrating," Lin said. "But maybe April just blocked out some time for personal reasons. From what you said, it's really only been a full day that she's been out of contact."

"Almost two days now." Heather's phone buzzed in her bag and she reached for it. "Oh, thank heavens. It's Leah. April called her. She's on the mainland in Harwich Port. The ferry back to the island was canceled last night so April couldn't get back. She's at the dock waiting to board the ferry now."

"That's a relief," Lin let out a breath. She was afraid the incoming text to Heather might be bad news.

"Does Leah say why April went to the mainland?" Viv asked.

"She doesn't. I'm sure she'll tell me later. She must be so thankful. Poor Leah." Heather's shoulders relaxed. "I think I'd like that coffee now, if you don't mind," she smiled at Viv.

When Viv returned with the coffee and a plate of muffins for everyone to share, conversation turned to island happenings and upcoming events.

"Labor Day will be here in a few weeks," Anton pointed out.

"Why does the summer always go by so quickly," Libby lamented.

"It's always been my favorite season," Lin told them. "Although, every season has its beauty."

"I love summer, too," Heather shared, "but I'm eternally grateful for air conditioning."

The others laughed.

"That's for certain," Anton agreed. "Well, I must be off. I have a meeting at the historical society. I'm very glad the young woman called to report where she's been. Have a good rest of the day, everyone." The older man gathered his things, stood, and rushed away.

"I apologize for taking up your time with my worries." Heather sipped from her coffee mug and then turned her attention to Lin and Viv. "Could I ask for your help? Would you talk to April about the messages? See if she'll tell you anything? Lori could introduce you."

Lin and Viv shared a quick glance.

"I guess we could, sure," Lin said. "We wouldn't want April to think we're ganging up on her though. Maybe we could meet Lori and April at a pub some night and the topic could come up in conversation."

"That would be great. I know Leah would appreciate it."

Lin met her landscaping partner at a client's house. Nicky jumped out of the truck and dashed over to the man. In his sixties, Leonard Reed was tall with muscular shoulders and arms, due to decades of outdoor labor. When Lin had arrived back on Nantucket after years away and met Leonard for the first time, she was sure he was a suspect in a murder case, and when she realized her mistake, she was sorry she'd had such unfounded suspicions about the man.

A few years ago, Lin suggested to Leonard that they join forces and start their own landscaping business together. Since then, they'd developed a reputation as one of the best gardeners and landscape designers on the island.

"Did you enjoy your few hours off, Coffin?"

Leonard asked as he hauled a small tree from the back of his truck and set it in a wheelbarrow. "Don't worry about abandoning me to do all the work alone in this heat and humidity."

A little smile formed over Lin's face. "I stopped at the bookstore for a little while."

"Did you bring me anything?" Leonard adjusted the tree in the wheelbarrow so it wouldn't fall out.

"How about an iced coffee and a cinnamon roll?" Lin went to the truck and got the drink and sweet treat.

"That's almost enough to forgive you for abandoning me. Almost." He gratefully took the large iced coffee and sipped through the straw.

"Why don't we sit in the shade and you can take a break," Lin suggested.

They and the dog walked to the edge of the property and sat on the grass under some mature shade trees. Leonard leaned against the trunk and took in a deep breath. "About ten degrees cooler in the shade."

"You know, you can take a break without me having to suggest it," Lin kidded.

"Can I?"

Nicky rested on the lawn right next to the man and Leonard patted the dog's soft fur.

"How was the visit to the antique house?"

Lin gave her friend the rundown on what happened while visiting the Main Street home with Jeff. "It was such a mournful sound. It cut right into my bones."

"I don't like hearing that." Leonard frowned. "Why doesn't the ghost cross over and leave the misery behind?"

"Something holds him back. Something he can't let go of." Lin ran her hand over the blades of green grass. "I'll need to find out what it is. If I can."

"If anyone can, it's you, Coffin."

"I'll go by the house when the workers aren't there. The new owners are renting a house on-island until the reno is done. Jeff told me they visit their new house only now and then since there isn't a whole lot to see just yet. I'm sure they'll go by more frequently once the work gets fully underway."

"It's good you can have some time alone in the place." Leonard bit into the cinnamon roll and sighed with delight and appreciation. "This is just what I needed. Caffeine and sugar. I can go on living."

Lin laughed. "You're welcome."

"Let's sit here a little while longer," he suggested.

"Heather came by when I was at the bookstore."

"Oh?" Leonard could tell by the tone of Lin's voice that there was something more to be said.

"She was concerned that her friend's daughter hadn't been in contact for a day and a half. Heather told us that was way out of character for the young woman. While we were sitting together, she got a text from her friend reporting her daughter was on the mainland and was about to return home. A canceled ferry last night prevented the daughter from getting back home."

"All's well that ends well, I guess," Leonard said. "I'm glad to hear there was a happy ending."

"There's something more. The young woman has been receiving some odd messages, almost threatening in tone."

An expression of worry crossed Leonard's face. "What's her name?"

"April Blake."

Leonard shook his head. "I know her father, Jim. He's a good guy. This business of strange messages has been going on for about eight years."

"What?" Lin stared at her friend. "Eight years?"

"Yeah. Jim and Leah have four daughters. April is the youngest. The other three live on the mainland now. Back years ago, the messages started and were directed mostly to the older girl. I guess she was eighteen at the time. Sometimes the notes were addressed to all four of the sisters. When Julie left Nantucket for college, the middle sisters got the brunt of the notes. When they left for school, the attention focused on April. The messages stopped when April went off to college. She came back home about a year ago."

"Did the police get involved?" Lin asked.

"Sure. But nothing ever came of it."

"What kinds of messages did they get?"

"Things about how the girls looked, how nice they were. Plenty of stuff about what the girls were doing, clubs they'd joined, athletic things they were involved with. Things like that. There was never anything threatening, but the weirdness of it all put the whole family on edge."

"And now, it's started again."

Leonard made eye contact with Lin. "I know you're going to be busy with this new ghost, but maybe you could talk to the family about these messages. Maybe you could pick up something about what's going on."

"Unless it's a ghost who's harassing them, I doubt I can figure out anything about the messages."

"Couldn't hurt. You and Viv have strong intuition. You might be able to apply your skills to the living, and not just to the dead."

"The dead keep me pretty busy." Lin looked sideways at her friend. "But we'll talk to them. And hopefully, we won't sense anything at all."

4

The next evening, Lin and Viv met with Anton at his antique Cape-style house located in a pretty neighborhood at the edge of town. Sitting at the long wooden table in front of the unlit fireplace in the cozy kitchen of Anton's house, they discussed what the historian had discovered about the haunted Colonial on upper Main Street. A platter in the middle of the table held slices of banana bread and chocolate chip cookies and they each had a tall glass of iced tea with ice cubes clinking against the sides.

"I haven't found a whole lot, but at least it's a starting point." Anton had notebooks and hard cover books scattered all over the table. He peered at his laptop as he tapped at the keys. "Here we are. The land the house sits on was originally owned by

Thackery Bean in the 1670s. The land was sold a number of times, but wasn't developed until George Bean repurchased it in 1834. He had the big house built that same year and it was passed from generation to generation until the most recent sale took place this year."

"The family held the house for nearly two-hundred years," Lin marveled.

"So the ghost must be a member of the Bean family?" Viv asked as she lifted her glass of iced tea to her lips.

Anton looked to Lin for an answer to the question.

"I don't know. Plenty of Bean family members must have died in the house over the years. The ghost could have been one of them. The sounds I heard when I was in the house made me think the ghost was a young man ... late teens or early twenties. Maybe he caught a disease and passed away in the home."

"It is certainly possible," Anton said. "There were two flu epidemics, along with typhus, typhoid, yellow fever. And that was just in the 1830s."

"Someone could have just died from old age and came back as a ghost," Viv offered.

"And he doesn't have to be a Bean family

member," Lin pointed out. "It could have been a guest, a friend, a housekeeper, someone who broke into the house." She looked at Anton. "Do you know anything else?"

"Not yet, but I'll go to the historical society tomorrow morning and search through their documents. First, I'll look for anything that might indicate an unusual cause of death. You never know what you can turn up. When will you visit the house again?"

"We're going there right after we leave here."

"I really think it would be better to go during the day," Viv brought up the suggestion for the fourth or fifth time.

"The workers will be there during most of the daytime hours. The renovation work is going to start up in earnest now," Lin said. "Jeff gave me an extra key. We have to go when the place is empty."

Viv sighed. "I really prefer to do these things when it's daylight."

Lin changed the subject to discuss April Blake and the messages she'd been getting.

"We're meeting with the Blake family tomorrow." She shared what Leonard told her about the unusual letters and messages that had been sent to the sisters over the past eight years.

33

"What? Eight years? Why haven't the police taken a closer look at this?" Viv's voice held a tone of outrage. "How can they allow this harassment to go on and on?"

"It's a strange series of events." Anton removed his glasses, rubbed the bridge of his nose, and then slipped the glasses back on. "How can the perpetrator keep up his interest in bothering the Blakes for eight years? Does the man have a grudge he's been fostering for nearly a decade? Is he in love with the sisters? What on earth drives a person to continue something like this for so many years?"

"Good questions," Lin shrugged.

"Could he know the sisters from high school or a job?" Viv asked. "It's not a big island. They must have interacted with this person at some time."

"Maybe he himself doesn't even know why he's doing it." Lin ran her finger over the condensation on her glass. "Also, we don't know if it's a man. It could be a woman. Anyway, we'll get more information tomorrow evening."

"From one weird thing to the next," Viv sighed.

"You're both very generous to help out," Anton remarked.

Lin smiled at the man. "We can say the same thing about you. You always spend hours and hours doing research to help us with the ghosts. We're very grateful."

Anton's cheeks tinged pink. "If not for you two and Libby, I would lead a very uninteresting life."

Viv chuckled. "Sometimes, that actually sounds very appealing."

After leaving Anton's house, the cousins strolled through the neighborhoods until they reached upper Main Street and approached the haunted Colonial.

"It looks creepy at night," Viv observed.

Lin poked her cousin with her elbow. "No, it doesn't. You're just worked up about going inside."

"It's so dark."

"The house has electricity, you know," Lin joked as they moved up the brick walkway to the front door.

"Aren't you a little wary? You heard the weeping when you were here before and it made you sad. Aren't you the least, tiny bit uneasy about going inside?"

"I am uneasy, but by focusing on you and your fears, I don't have to obsess over my own."

"It's a good thing I'm here then."

Lin unlocked the front door and went inside where she flipped the switch and lit up the foyer.

"It's a big house," Viv said as they walked around the rooms. "Where did the candlestick go flying?"

"Right here. This used to be a sitting room."

Viv took hold of her cousin's arm. "I see the dent in the wall."

"There's more than one."

"Hopefully, no new dents get put there tonight ... or in my head," Viv said with apprehension.

"Next time, we can bring helmets. There are still some pieces of furniture left from the previous owners," Lin pointed out. "Some nice pieces. They look like antiques."

"Maybe the new owners requested that some of the things were to be conveyed with the house," Viv suggested.

Thump, thump, thump.

"Oh gosh, what's that?" Viv glanced up to the ceiling.

"Footsteps," Lin said softly. "We have company. Or I guess we're the ones who are the visitors since the ghost lives here."

"Is he going to stay upstairs? He isn't going to come down here, is he?"

"He stayed upstairs the first time I was here. If he doesn't come down, eventually I'll have to go up."

"Why?" Viv looked at her cousin like she'd lost her mind.

"I need to try and communicate with him. If he won't come to me, then I'll have to go to him."

"But he could be dangerous. He's already thrown things around. Maybe you should wait until Jeff is with you."

A chair in the corner of the room began to jiggle in place.

Viv shifted her position to stand behind Lin. "What's going on? What's going on with the chair?"

Lin kept her eyes on the ceiling. "It's me. Lin Coffin. I promised to come back. This is my cousin Viv. She helps me help spirits."

"Oh gosh," Viv whispered. "Maybe it would be better if you don't call attention to me."

"Would you like to appear to us?" Lin waited for the ghost to respond.

Knocking sounds started on the second floor, softly at first and then slowly getting louder. They seemed to be coming from the room overhead.

"Is he answering you by knocking?" Viv kept her voice soft and low.

"I don't know if it's a reply or it would have

started anyway." Lin walked around the room they were in, looking up at the ceiling. "The knocking seems to be coming from the room directly overhead. I think the weeping and moaning I heard last time was also coming from that room. Let's go upstairs and see which bedroom it is."

"Now?" Viv practically screeched. "Is that a good idea?"

"We'll find out." Lin headed for the staircase.

"You're not leaving me alone down here," Viv told her cousin as she hurried to catch up.

When they reached the landing, the knocking sounds ceased and Lin oriented herself to the second floor rooms by peeking into all of them.

"Look, the stairs go up to the third floor. On this level, there's a smaller bedroom, two large bedrooms, a sitting room, two bathrooms, and the biggest bedroom is right over here. This is where the sounds have been coming from. They seem to be localized right in this room."

Lin stepped in. There was a bedframe, an upholstered chair by the window, and a small wooden desk with cubby holes and a single drawer.

"The desk looks like an antique," Viv noted. "It's lovely."

"The rooms make me feel wistful," Lin sighed.

"The things left behind. The remains of someone's life, pushed into a corner. I hope the owners were happy here. I hope they had good lives."

A bang came from the far wall like something heavy had been flung against it, and both women jumped.

"What was that?" Viv glanced around.

A landline telephone stood on a small table near the bed. It rang.

"Should we answer it?" Viv asked.

"I'd think the phone would have been disconnected." Lin walked over to it and hesitated before picking up the receiver. "Hello?"

A click, and then nothing. Not even a dial tone.

"I think our ghost is playing tricks on us. It seems the phone *has been* disconnected."

"If he doesn't want to appear to you, then maybe he should talk to you by way of the phone." Viv shook her head and walked over to inspect the desk.

The women waited a few more minutes, but there were no shimmering particles to indicate a ghost was taking shape.

"I guess we should head out. We can visit again another day."

As they moved to the doorway, Lin reached for the wall switch to turn off the lights, but before she could touch it, she heard a soft scratching sound in the room.

She turned and noticed something on the desk.

Walking slowly to the beautiful antique, her eyes went wide. "Viv? Come here."

When Viv crossed the room to stand beside her cousin, Lin gestured to the desk. "Look at that."

A little gasp escaped from Viv's throat.

There was a heavy piece of writing parchment on the desk ... and a pen was suspended in the air as if an invisible hand was moving it over the paper.

5

"The ghost is writing?" Viv's voice was as soft as a murmur.

"He's moving the pen, but no words are showing on the paper."

"When I was looking at the desk a few minutes ago, there wasn't any paper on the desk. And no magical pen either," Viv said.

Suddenly, the cousins heard a man's and a woman's voice downstairs.

"Hello? Is someone upstairs?" the man called.

"It must be the new owners," Lin said. "Yes, we're up here. We're coming down."

Viv took hold of Lin's arm. "Look."

Lin turned her head back to the desk. The paper and pen were gone.

The man and woman came into the room.

"Hello. Who are you?" The man's expression was friendly.

"I'm Lin Coffin, and this is my cousin Viv. My husband Jeff is one of the owners of the renovation company you hired to work on the house. He gave me a key. He told me about the ... unusual activity in the house. Viv and I have some experience with such things."

"I see," the woman said. "I'm Eileen Salem. Nice to meet you both."

"I'm Michael Salem."

The couple appeared to be in their early to mid-sixties. Eileen was tall and slim, had short blond hair and big brown eyes. Michael looked like a runner ... tall, skinny... and he had gray hair and ice blue eyes.

They shook hands with the young women.

"What do you think of the situation?" Eileen asked. "We had a ghost in our previous home. It was harmless and left us alone for the most part."

Michael added, "When we first moved into that house, the spirit was quite active. I'd say a bit of a pest. Noises, cold air currents, things going missing. It was somewhat of a nuisance, but we behaved as though nothing bothered us and remained good-natured about it. Eventually, the ghost quieted down. We're hoping the same thing will happen here. Change can be upsetting ... even to spirits."

"You have very good attitudes about all of it," Lin smiled.

"Jeff told us he knew someone who could come by and scope out the situation," Michael said. "He didn't tell us it was his wife."

"Viv and I have been involved with a number of ghosts," Lin explained. "The skill runs in our family. Our ancestors were early settlers of the island."

"The Coffins," Eileen said.

"Yes, and the Witchards," Viv told them.

"Both some of the earliest families on Nantucket," Michael observed.

The four of them talked for a while about some island history, island living, and town news.

"There are some lovely pieces of furniture here in the house," Viv said. "Are they yours or did they come with the place?"

"All the pieces here came with the sale," Eileen said. "We specifically asked for them when we were negotiating with the seller's attorney."

"We came by to take some of them to our rental place. We don't want to leave them here while the renovation and restoration work is going on,"

Michael said. "We'll bring a van by in a few days to get the bigger pieces."

Lin glanced back to the desk. "Could you leave the desk in here for a little while longer?"

"Sure. I don't think the upstairs will be worked on right away," Eileen nodded. "The start of the work will be focused on the first floor."

"Is there something about the desk that you think is connected to the ghost?" Michael inquired.

"It's possible. I'd hate to lose a tie to the spirit. If you could leave it here just a bit longer, it might be very helpful," Lin said.

"We'd be glad to," Eileen smiled.

The next evening, Lin and Viv met with Leah, Jim, and April Blake at their sprawling farmhouse-style home. April was twenty-three, had long wavy strawberry-blond hair and green eyes. She had a warm, friendly, and unassuming manner that would put anyone at ease. Leah, fifty-eight, had auburn hair and was of medium build. She also had a warm, friendly, welcoming personality. Sixty-year-old Jim had broad shoulders, gray hair, a twinkle in his eye, and an easy smile.

They all sat outside on the patio to enjoy the pleasant evening weather.

"So, Heather Jenness tells us you both have some experience helping the police," Jim said as he passed around a tray of cheese and crackers.

"Well, we've only helped them once," Lin corrected, "but we do have some experience helping people with different things. We've been told we have good reasoning, analytical, and investigative skills." She smiled. "Though not everyone would agree with that assessment."

The others chuckled.

"Can you tell us about the messages you've received over the years?" Viv asked.

Jim let out a long breath and told the tale, with his wife and daughter adding comments.

"It's sure a strange story," Lin said. "You mentioned putting up a security camera that turned on when it detected motion. Why do you think it never caught the person?"

Jim leaned back in his seat. "Most messages are left in the mailbox. Maybe it was just out of range of the camera's reach. We talked about moving the camera, but that would require us putting up a pole in the front yard to anchor the camera on it. None of us wanted to do that."

Leah said, "We felt like putting up a pole would give the *Mailman* some measure of satisfaction that he was successful in rattling us. That's what we've called him over the years, the Mailman."

"We've all taken turns staying up all night to watch for him," April reported. "None of us have ever seen him."

"It must be coincidence that he's been able to elude detection?" Lin asked. "I mean, he wouldn't be able to tell someone was in the house awake all night, watching for him."

"I think that's the only logical explanation," Jim said.

"Did you notice any seasonal fluctuations to the messages?" Lin questioned. "Did they only appear in the summer?"

"We wondered if the person was on-island only at certain times of the year," Viv noted.

"The summer has always been the most active time for the Mailman," Leah explained. "But messages are left during the other seasons as well."

"So it's probably not a seasonal visitor," Lin observed. "There could be reasons why the summer is the busiest time. Maybe he's a teacher and has the summer off and that gives him more time to deliver his messages. Being a teacher might have given him interaction with your daughters when they were in school."

"We've talked about that as a possibility," Jim said.

"Are the messages always typed?"

"Some are handwritten," April said, "but mostly they look to be printed from a computer."

The cousins nodded.

"Have you ever had a dog?" Lin asked the family.

"We had a dog for years. He passed away a few months before April returned to the island."

"The dog never barked or alerted you to someone outside?" Viv wondered.

Jim shook his head. "He was a friendly animal. He'd bark on occasion, but it never led to us seeing the Mailman."

"When did you come back to Nantucket?" Lin asked April.

"About eight months ago. I had a part-time job doing design work after I graduated from college, but I missed the island and wanted to come home."

"You attended art school?"

"I did. I have a small business making Nantucket baskets."

"Do you live here at home?" Viv asked.

"I have an apartment on the edge of town." April

smiled at her parents. "My mom and dad own the building and I rent one of the apartments from them. I don't think I could afford to live here if not for them."

"We help each other out," Leah told them. "Jim and I have been fortunate. We have the restaurant, some real estate holdings. It's the least we can do to give our daughter a hand while she's starting out."

April chuckled. "I'm the starving artist. My sisters all chose smart professions. Julie has one more year to finish medical school, Molly just graduated from law school, and Mallory is an accountant."

"That doesn't matter. You have to choose the path that's right for you," Leah said. "Once you get established as an artist, you'll be off and running."

"We heard you have a social media following," Viv said.

April almost looked sheepish. "That all happened by accident. I started posting videos of me making my baskets. I'd give some history about Nantucket while I worked. I talked about the history of the baskets. Sometimes, I'd post videos of places on the island and toss in some historical tidbits. My stuff took off. Now I feel pressure to keep it up ... to make the content better. It takes quite a while to video and edit a segment, plus thinking up interesting segments. It has helped my online basket business, but honestly, I wasn't prepared for the attention."

"Did the Mailman start up with the messages around the same time your social media presence took off?" Lin asked.

"He started about three weeks after I got home, so no, it wasn't social media that caused him to start up again." A shadow flitted over April's face.

"Since you're not living at home, do the messages arrive at your apartment?" Viv questioned.

"Most of them still get put in my parents' mailbox. I did get two messages at my apartment mailbox. I think he wanted me to know that he knew where I was living." April's shoulders slumped.

"We think it must be easier for him to deliver to our mailbox," Jim said.

"He might think it would be easier to identify him if he delivers to April's mailbox," Leah's face hardened. "There are more people around at the apartment house than there are here."

"You've put up with this for a long time," Lin said.

"Honestly, I'm pretty tired of it," April admitted. "I considered moving off-island. I went to Harwich on the mainland the other day to look at a few apartments. I didn't tell anyone I was going because I hadn't decided if I was going to move or not. While I was there, I got angry and decided I wasn't going to give in to this creep's harassment and intimidation. I want to live here. So I'm staying."

"I copied some of the messages we've received over the years. We've kept most of them." Jim handed a manilla envelope to the cousins. "Take a look. See if any ideas pop into your head. We'd be very grateful for any assistance you can give us. But don't worry. There's no pressure. I have to admit we aren't hopeful."

6

——————

Lin, Jeff, Viv, and John took their paddleboards, towels, and a couple of coolers to the area between Steps and Jetties beaches. The sky was a beautiful blue and the day was hot, but with low humidity. A perfect day for the beach.

Wearing a dog-sized life vest, Nicky rode at the end of Jeff's board like a captain steering his ship. If a little wave came over the front, the dog would bark happily and wag his little tail so fast that it looked like a propeller.

After paddling along the shore, Lin and Viv sat down on their boards to chat and soak up the sun while the guys kept going.

"Do you think the ghost is going to actually write

some words on a piece of paper one of these days?" Viv asked.

"I don't know what to think." Lin splashed some seawater on her face to cool down. "I didn't get much sleep last night. I couldn't turn off my mind. Thoughts about the ghost went round and round in my head."

"If the ghost does write something, I'm sure it will be cryptic and hard to figure out, but at least, it would be *something* to go on."

"Because of the distress sounds he made the first time I was there, it has me leaning toward a traumatic experience that must have happened that keeps him at the house and prevents him from crossing over."

"The death of his child or wife?" Viv asked.

"The ghost sounds young so I don't think that's it. It has to be loss of some other kind."

Jeff and John paddled over to the women.

"How's Nicky enjoying the ride?" Lin asked as she reached over to pat the dog.

"He loves it." Jeff sat on his board and let it float next to his wife and Viv.

"You look serious," John said to the cousins. "You must be talking about the latest ghost."

"Or the problems the Blakes have been having with those strange messages," Jeff pointed out.

"I heard about that ghostly pen writing invisible words on the piece of paper last night." John shook his head. "This stuff is so hard to believe, but I have to admit, it would be cool to see something like that."

Lin smiled. "You're welcome to join the investigation at any time."

"Why don't you just video the pen on your phone and show me later?" John suggested.

Viv used her hand to splash some water in her husband's direction. "We're trying to solve the case, not create entertainment."

"But you could do both," John teased, and hit the water with his hand so it would spray on Viv.

Lin stood and lifted her paddle. "Okay, I'm heading back to shore before this water splashing turns into a war."

Back on the beach, they sat in sand chairs under the umbrellas and Viv opened the cooler and handed out the sandwiches, pasta salad, cut-up carrots, and cold drinks.

"You haven't told me the content of the notes that have been sent to the Blakes." John munched on his chicken sandwich.

"We don't really know anything much." Lin passed Jeff a thermos of water. "Jim Blake gave us an envelope with copies of the notes, but we haven't looked at them yet."

"That's tonight's task, after dinner," Viv remarked.

After lunch, they played corn hole on the beach, swam in the ocean, sunned themselves on the blankets, and then headed to their homes.

Once they showered, Viv and John walked to Lin's house to gather for dinner. Lin had inherited her Nantucket cottage from her grandfather. The place was designed in a unique "U" shape. One wing housed the master bedroom and a bathroom, and the living room was located in the center. A second bedroom that Lin used as an office was off the living space. The kitchen and dining area and another bathroom was found in the other leg of the "U." The living room and kitchen had big windows and doors that led out to the large deck, and beyond that was a patio which overlooked a natural area of trees and brush. Lin and Jeff had been renovating the upstairs of the house where there would be an office for Jeff, two more bedrooms, two bathrooms, and a sitting area. They were making progress, but the work went slowly since they only had free time in the evenings and on weekends.

Nicky greeted Viv and John at the front door, and when Viv placed Queenie on the floor, the cat and dog used the kitchen doggie door to dash outside into the yard.

Lin poured drinks for everyone and they went out to the deck where Jeff was preparing the grill for chicken, steak, and veggie kabobs. A salad and a bowl of rice had been placed in the center of the big deck table and four place settings had been set with white plates, glasses, napkins, and cutlery.

"It's perfect weather," Viv said. "I might even need a sweater later on."

"I'm so glad the humidity broke. It's been killing me working outside the past few days." Lin opened a bottle of sparkling water and poured some into the glasses.

"That's why I chose a job where I can work inside in an air-conditioned space," Viv smiled.

"I should just do remote software programming and sell the landscaping business," Lin joked. She still did some occasional remote programming for a company she used to work for that was located on the mainland.

"That'll be the day. You love landscaping. And

you wouldn't leave Leonard to do it on his own." John opened a bottle of beer and took a long swallow.

Lin laughed. "You know me too well. I like being outside."

Jeff turned the foil-wrapped corn on the cob on the grill and checked the kabobs. "Everything will be done in a few minutes."

John talked about some new houses he'd recently listed and Jeff told them about the renovation projects he and Kurt had going on.

"Some guys are a little leery about working at the house on Main Street. They know Nantucket is known for ghosts, but that doesn't mean they want to work somewhere with odd things going on." Jeff shook his head. "It's making it hard to schedule all the projects we have right now. We have to be careful who we send where. We don't want anyone quitting on us."

"I wouldn't work in that house." John took another drink of his beer. "I know I'm a coward, but I have a strong sense of self-preservation. I don't need to get hit in the head with a candlestick." He smiled. "Even though it might knock some sense into me." Changing the subject, John asked, "Want to go out on the boat tomorrow? It's supposed to be a nice day.

We can sail around the island or head toward the Vineyard."

"That sounds great," Jeff nodded. "We haven't been out on your boat for a couple of weeks."

"We can bring some leftovers from dinner tonight and have them for lunch on the boat," Lin suggested.

When the meal was over and the dishes cleaned up, they all sat around the kitchen table and Lin brought out the manila envelope Jim Blake had given them. She opened it and placed a stack of papers on the tabletop.

"These are copies Jim made of the original letters they received," Viv explained.

"The papers are numbered," Jeff pointed out. "They must be in chronological order."

"Shall I read them out loud?" Lin asked.

The others agreed.

"After the first ten letters were read, Lin stopped and looked up. "This is unnerving."

"I'll say." Jeff looked disgusted.

The letters were upbeat and complimentary of the Blake sisters ... how pretty they all were, how active in the community they were, how special each one was. The sender mentioned things the girls had been doing at school or in town, and named some of their friends.

"If these notes were sent by a grandparent or aunt, it might be okay," Lin said. "But from a stranger? It's downright stalking."

"It seems the police could have done more to stop it," Viv told them.

"It would take too much time for an officer to sit at the Blakes' house until the person came by and put something in the mailbox," John said. "It isn't a good use of their time."

Jeff agreed. "There are only a few officers and a whole island to manage."

"I think I would have taken the family and moved off-island," Viv said.

"That wouldn't be so easy to do. The Blakes's businesses are here," John pointed out.

"And they must have thought the person would get bored eventually and stop leaving the notes," Jeff suggested.

"There's only one handwritten note in the pile. The rest are printed from a computer," Lin said shuffling through the short letters. "From the phrasing of the notes and the handwriting, do you get a sense of how old the person might be?"

Viv gave her opinion first. "A middle-aged person."

"Why?" Lin asked.

Viv shrugged. "If it was a teen or young adult, the words he or she used would be a little different. It seems too formal ... a little stiff. It doesn't have the flow of a young person's language. And if the Mailman is someone much older than middle-age ... the language used would be different, way more formal."

"I think you're right," Jeff said.

Lin and John were also in agreement.

"So the Mailman, as the Blakes call him, might be someone who works at the school," Lin said.

"Do the Blakes go to church?" Viv asked. "It could be someone from the church they attend."

"I don't know. We can ask them."

"They own a restaurant in town," Jeff said. "The sisters probably worked there in the summers. They could have caught a customer's eye."

"The letters show up in all seasons, though mostly in the summer," Lin told them.

"So the person must own a house here," Viv guessed. "He or she might spend more time here in the summer. The Mailman might have to spend time off-island in the off-seasons."

"That makes sense," John said.

"This hasn't been solved in years." Lin shook her head. "We'll have to be awfully lucky to figure it out."

"Or ... we'll figure it out when he escalates and does something awful," Viv suggested.

Nicky growled, Queenie hissed, and the people around the table groaned.

7

It had been a fun day out on the water on John's sailboat with Jeff, Lin, Viv, and John enjoying the sun and breeze, swimming off the boat, and eating leftovers from dinner the previous night. Now, the sun had set and they were sitting on the boat's deck moored at the town dock eating homemade pizza and watching the tourists and townsfolk strolling past the boats.

Nicky and Queenie were perched together on a large lounge chair, napping and occasionally looking around at the people walking past. Reassured nothing was amiss, they'd go back to sleep.

"Another glass of wine?" John asked Lin.

"I'd better not. All the swimming and fresh air

today has knocked me out. If I have another glass, I'll have to go below and fall asleep on the bed."

"You can always just nap in your chair," Viv suggested. "I'll wake you up when it's time to go home."

"Or you can stay awake and have some home-made ice cream," John told her.

Lin sat straight in her chair. "Homemade ice cream?"

"That perked her up," Jeff laughed.

"What flavor?" Lin stared at John.

"Two flavors. Pistachio or vanilla."

"What about a scoop of each?"

"We can do that." John got up and went below. He was back in a few minutes with a tray containing two cartons of ice cream, whipped cream, sprinkles, glass bowls, napkins, and spoons.

"When did you learn to make ice cream?" Jeff helped his friend scoop.

"A few days ago. I decided I wanted to learn, so I did." John put a dollop of whipped cream on Lin's ice cream. "And it came out really well."

Viv put a spoonful of rainbow sprinkles on her scoops of vanilla.

"This is delicious." Lin held her spoon up to her lips and licked it. "I'm definitely awake now."

"So more wine then?" John chuckled.

"How about coffee instead?"

"Coming right up." John went below once again and on his return, he brought up coffee for everyone.

"I love sitting on this boat in the evening watching the people." Jeff balanced his ice cream bowl in his lap while he took a sip of his coffee. "The docks look beautiful under the night sky."

John said, "Come down any night. I'm almost always here."

"It's true," Viv smiled. "He's always here. If I want to see my husband in the summer, I have to come down to the boat."

"Luckily, I have an understanding wife."

Viv and John got out their guitars and played some songs while they all sang along. When they did a cover of a song that was popular on the radio, a crowd gathered on the dock and the people clapped to the music and joined in singing on the chorus. When the last note played, everyone applauded and cheered before they went on their way.

"Well, that was unexpected." Viv chuckled and set down her guitar.

"Maybe we should put out a container for donations," John smiled.

Lin said, "Maybe we'll get ticketed for disturbing the peace."

"The police will stuff all four of us into the tiny holding cell," Viv told them.

John looked at his wife and raised an eyebrow. "How do you know how big the holding cell is?"

"You know Lin and I were wild in our younger days," Viv winked.

"Leonard told us," Lin clarified. "You know he spent some time in the holding cell back in the day when he'd had too much to drink."

"I'm sure glad those days are over," John said. "He's a new man now."

"All thanks to Lin," Jeff smiled at her.

Lin shook her head. "Leonard was the one who decided to make a change."

"Yes, because of your friendship with him," Jeff insisted.

"Jeff's right," Viv agreed. "If you hadn't come back to the island, who knows what would have happened to Leonard."

"You're giving me way too much credit." Lin glanced over to the small stores lining the sidewalk on the docks, and she set her coffee mug on the table. At the corner of one of the shops, the ghosts of

Lin's ancestors, Sebastian and Emily, stood shimmering in the lights, looking in her direction.

Noticing her cousin's expression, Viv asked, "Are you okay? Lin?"

Lin shook herself. "It's Sebastian and Emily. They're standing over by the leather goods shop."

Three pairs of eyes followed Lin's gaze.

"I don't see anything," John said. "Not surprisingly."

"I might see some sparkles, but it could just be the bright lights." Jeff squinted trying to make out the ghosts.

"I don't see them either," Viv leaned back in her chair.

"You don't see them because you don't want to," Lin told her cousin.

"What are they doing?" Viv questioned.

"Just looking at me." Lin slowly raised her hand in greeting.

"They're here because of the Main Street ghost," Viv guessed. "Are they trying to tell you something?"

"I can't tell yet."

"If we all stop chattering," John said, "Lin might be able to receive a message of some sort."

In a matter of moments, everything around Lin went still as if all the sounds had moved far, far away.

The hubbub of all the people strolling about slowly faded, and Sebastian and Emily began to glow. Reaching for her necklace, Lin rubbed her finger over the little horseshoe.

Is there something you want to tell me? Lin thought the message without using spoken words.

Emily glanced away from the docks and looked toward the town.

Sebastian stared into her eyes and a word formed in Lin's mind.

Danger.

Lin whispered, "Something's wrong." Immediately, her phone buzzed with an incoming text.

Lin, it's April Blake. I just got a new note from the Mailman. It's threatening. I hate to ask, but can you come by? I'm afraid.

"I need to go to April's place." Lin stood. "She just got another note. She's frightened."

"I'm coming." As Viv grabbed her sweater, Nicky and Queenie jumped to their feet.

"No one's going anywhere without me." Jeff stood, too.

"Do you want me to come?" John asked. "Safety in numbers."

"It wouldn't hurt," Jeff told him.

"Queenie, stay here," Viv said to the cat.

Nicky jumped to the dock and trotted ahead with the humans following after.

"Did April say what the message said?" Jeff asked.

"She didn't. Whatever it was, it seems to have rattled her like never before." Lin felt adrenaline coursing through her body.

"How long does this torment have to go on?" Viv complained. "The family has been put through the wringer for years. Something has to be done. The police have to take this more seriously."

"Whatever is in this new message," Jeff said, "it might prompt them to act."

"Or maybe a private investigator needs to be hired," John suggested. "Has the family ever considered hiring one?"

"I don't know." Lin felt shaky as she hurried along the brick sidewalks to the street where April was living.

When they approached the house, April came out and stood on the porch. "Thank heavens, you're here." A few tears slipped from the young woman's eyes and she brushed them away.

When Nicky trotted up the steps to the woman and rubbed his head against her leg, April bent down and patted him. The dog's presence seemed to calm her.

Lin introduced the men and then said, "What happened?"

April shoved a piece of paper into Lin's hand. "Read it."

After her eyes had read every word on the computer-printed short note, Lin read the message aloud.

The young man you went out with last night isn't worthy of you. You are far too good for him. I'm asking you to stop seeing him. You deserve far better. Also I don't think it's a good idea for you to be living alone in an apartment. You need to go back to staying with your parents. Listen to me, April, or you will regret it. I only want what's best for you.

"He threatened me." April's jaw was tight and a muscle in her face twitched. Her hands were clenched by her sides. "I should get a gun."

Viv's eyes widened. "That might not be the best idea. Do you carry pepper spray?"

"I have some." April nodded.

"But do you carry it with you?" Viv pressed. "It doesn't do any good at the bottom of your purse or sitting on top of your dresser."

"I'll carry it."

"Did you see anyone at the mailbox?" Lin questioned.

"No. I went to dinner with a friend and checked the box when I got back."

"Did you notice anyone paying attention to you ... watching you ... someone's gaze lingering a little too long?"

"I didn't." April ran her hand through her hair. "I should be more aware."

"I think you should take this to the police. Unlike the previous notes, this one has a veiled threat in it. Let the police take a look at it. Let them decide what to do." Lin looked at the big old house. "What floor do you live on?"

"The first."

"Are there other apartments on the first floor?"

"One other. There are five apartments in the house, two on the first, two on the second, and one on the third."

"Do you know the other first floor tenant?"

"It's a young guy. We've met. He seems nice."

"Would you consider going to your parents' house for a few days?"

"I already packed a bag, but I don't want the Mailman to think I'm doing what he told me to do, so I'm reconsidering leaving my place. I'd rather stay here."

"Do you have a friend who could come and stay for a couple of days?"

"I can call my friend. She'll come."

"You went out with someone last night?" Lin asked.

"It was just a casual thing. A guy came by to purchase a Nantucket basket for his mom's birthday. We got to talking and he suggested we go to get a bite to eat. It makes my skin crawl to know I'm being watched by the Mailman." She placed a hand on her stomach. "It makes me feel sick."

"We understand," Viv told her. "It's a violation."

"Would you call your friend and ask if she can come to stay the night?" Lin asked. "I don't want to leave you alone. We'll wait until she shows up."

"I'll text right now." April's thumbs flew over the screen of her phone. "Lauren's dependable and a good friend."

Lin, Viv, Jeff, John, and Nicky sat on the porch with April and chatted together until her friend showed up.

On the walk back to the boat, John said, "Maybe we should take turns hiding in the bushes outside

April's house at night waiting for the creep to show up."

"It's not a bad idea," Jeff agreed. "I'd do it."

"There's something that's bothering me," Viv said.

"What's that?" Lin asked.

"I bet the Mailman was watching us at April's. What if he starts stalking *us*? Or worse?"

Nicky growled.

And a shiver ran over Lin's skin.

8

Lin and Viv made their way to the library section of the historical museum.

"Researching today?" Felix Harper, the museum's librarian asked. The man was an encyclopedia of information about Nantucket history. He knew almost as much as Anton. Tall and thin, with salt and pepper hair and blue eyes, Felix was always well-dressed and fashionable. He was wearing nicely-tailored gray slacks, a crisp white shirt with a blue tie, and a fitted navy blazer.

"Would you like me to set you up on the computers and point you to the digital newspapers?"

Lin and Viv were frequent visitors to the library and often requested access to the digital newspapers.

"We'd like to look at them, yes," Lin smiled at the

man, grateful to have such a helpful person to deal with.

"What date range?" Felix sat down at a bank of computers.

"Well, the house and people we're interested in are between the 1830s and the present," Viv explained.

"You'll be sitting here for a few weeks in order to go through all of that data," Felix chuckled. "Starting from 1830 or from today's date and going backward?"

"We'd like to start with the oldest material first." Lin sat down next to the man.

Felix tapped away. "Which house's history are you looking into?"

Lin gave him the address.

"The Bean House. There's a ghost in that house, you know." Felix slid over to prepare the next computer so each cousin could work on her own.

Lin's eyes went wide. "A ghost? How do you know that?"

"A friend of mine mentioned it."

"What did your friend say?" Viv looked at the librarian with a wary expression.

"Only that the house was haunted."

"How does he know that?"

"He's an art dealer. He went there years ago to

speak to the owners. They had a painting they wanted to sell. He told me the woman who lived there mentioned a ghost. He thought it was amusing."

"Did the owner say why she thought there was a ghost in her house?" Lin was surprised by the news.

"If she did, my friend didn't share the information with me. He doesn't believe such things."

"But," Viv said, "this is Nantucket. Lots of people here believe there are ghosts present."

"Not my friend." Felix stood. "You're all set. If you need any help, just come and get me."

The cousins sat down in front of the computers.

"So, the former owners knew there was a ghost in their house," Lin said quietly. "I wonder when the ghost passed away. His passing must have been traumatic in some way. Most angry ghosts have a traumatic event in their past. From our experiences, contented spirits who don't cross over remain in a house due to happy memories."

"Well, you sense that he's young, late teens to early twenties," Viv said. "His angst probably isn't due to losing his child. Maybe his girlfriend died?"

"Our ghost was too young to have owned a place like that so his girlfriend probably didn't die in the Main Street house. So why would he remain there? What tie would there be to keep him in the house?"

Viv shrugged. "Good points. Maybe he died in the house from whatever disease was circulating at the time. He died young and couldn't deal with it, and so, is stuck there."

"That's a very plausible idea." Lin started to tap on the keyboard. "We have a lot of information to sift through. It won't be easy to find him. And his last name might not even be Bean. His mother might have been a member of the Bean family which would mean he had his father's last name. I guess the first thing we should look for is a list of owners of the Main Street house. That will give us names to search for." Lin looked around. "I should have thought of this first. I'll go find Felix and ask him where to look for that kind of information."

An hour later, Felix was able to produce a list of the house's owners and Lin and Viv searched for information on a few of the residents. Some had barely a mention here and there, some had nothing at all.

Lin rubbed the back of her neck and checked the time on her phone. "We should head out. Jeff said the restoration work at the house would end by this time and we'll be able to pay a visit without anyone around."

"Fine by me." Viv blinked several times. "I wonder if I need reading glasses. My eyes get so tired after staring at a screen for so long." She pulled some visual lubricant from her bag and applied it to her eyes. "Let's stop by the bookstore before we go to the house. We can pick up some iced coffees to take with us."

Lin's face brightened. "I'd love that. And maybe a muffin, too."

"I think that can be arranged."

The young women packed up their things, walked to the bookstore, got the drinks and sweets, and strolled to upper Main Street. As they approached the house, Eileen and Michael Salem came out from the front door and stopped by the street to speak with them.

"Hello." Eileen greeted the cousins with a smile. "Coming by to visit our resident spirit?"

"We thought it would be a good time to stop by. My husband told me the day's work would be finished by now," Lin reported.

"The men left about twenty minutes ago. They were packing up when we got here," Michael said. "We put a couple of pieces of furniture into our van."

Lin's face dropped and Eileen noticed.

"Don't worry," she said. "We left the desk upstairs. It's right where it's always been."

"We appreciate that," Viv nodded.

"We could hear footsteps upstairs," Eileen said.

"We also heard things being tossed around and shattering." Michael let out a sigh. "Nothing's broken. It's just the ghost making noise. Be careful when you go in. The spirit seems agitated today."

Lin noticed some flickering near the front door of the house and was surprised to see Sebastian and Emily standing there. She concentrated on them in case they were trying to send her a message, but nothing came through.

"Lin?" Viv asked.

Lin blinked and turned. "Sorry, I got distracted. What did you say?"

Eileen spoke, "We asked if you know of a way to calm down the spirit."

"Not exactly. There's no science to it. We just try to understand what the ghost wants."

"I see. Well, good luck with it."

"We'd better get going," Michael said. "We have guests coming this evening."

The couple headed for their van.

"We'll see you soon." Eileen waved.

"Shall we go in?" Viv asked.

"Emily and Sebastian are here," Lin shared. "They're near the front of the house."

"Did they communicate?" Viv looked at the big house.

"No, but they must want to."

"Should we go toward them or wait right here for some message?"

"Let's stay still for a minute." Lin kept her eyes pinned on her ancestors, waiting for a sign, or a word, or *something* from them. Slowing her breathing, she attempted to clear her mind to keep the communication channels open.

The tiny, shimmering particles that made up both ghosts began to fade, and in a moment, they were gone.

"Nothing. They left." Lin sounded disappointed at the lack of a message.

"Maybe next time." Viv said encouragingly.

Inside the antique house, they set their drinks on the counter in the outdated kitchen.

Viv ran her hand over the old cabinetry. "When the restoration is done, this house is going to be a showplace."

"I can't wait to see it in its finished state."

A loud crash startled the women.

"Jeez." Viv looked up at the ceiling. "Someone's got a bee in his bonnet today."

Lin couldn't help but chuckle, but then she jumped again at the next smashing sound. They hurried into the first floor sitting room. Most of the noise was coming from overhead. It sounded like one glass object after another was being thrown across the room upstairs and was smashing against the walls.

Lin had to raise her voice over the din. "Let's go up to the second floor."

Giving her cousin a wary look, Viv agreed and they climbed the stairs to the upper floor landing where the terrible sounds were much louder.

Viv leaned close to Lin so she could be heard over the crashing and smashing sounds. "I should have brought my noise-canceling headphones."

With a smile, Lin nodded.

They shuffled closer to the main bedroom and peeked inside. The room was empty and nothing could be seen broken or smashed anywhere in the room despite all the noise coming from the space.

When Lin took a step into the room, the noise abruptly stopped.

Before either one could say anything, the sounds of doors opening and closing, phones ringing, footsteps stomping, and knocking on the walls filled the air.

"I thought it was over," Viv shouted and clapped her hands over her ears.

Lin raised her voice. "It's me, Lin. Viv is here, too. What's upsetting you today? Can you appear to us? Will you try to communicate with us? We want to help."

The noises stopped.

Lin stepped further into the room and Viv followed.

"We're trying to understand what you need," Lin continued. "We hope we can do something for you."

Silence.

"Can you appear to us?"

Nothing.

They heard the sounds of footsteps running across the room.

"Can you tell us your name somehow? Sometimes spirits send me a mental message. Would you like to try?"

Lin and Viv turned to the right when they heard the sounds of knocking on the wall, and Lin walked to the side of the room and placed her hand on it. She closed her eyes, hoping the knocking might be a way to receive a message.

Morse code? It didn't sound like that's what it was.

"Lin." Viv gestured to the small desk near the window where a pen was suspended in mid-air.

Hurrying over, Lin saw a piece of paper on the desktop. "Can you write a word for us?"

The pen trembled, and then it and the piece of paper disappeared.

Disappointment crossed the cousins' faces.

"It seemed close. It seemed like he was going to write something." Lin kept staring at the desk.

Viv put her arm around Lin's shoulders. "It's okay. Things take time. We'll come back. We'll keep trying. He'll do it eventually."

9

Lin and Viv stopped to pick up Nicky before heading to Viv's place for dinner. Jeff was working late and John was on the boat so the cousins had the house to themselves. Located in a neighborhood at the edge of town, Viv's antique Cape-style house had a white picket fence around the front yard that had red, white, and pink roses spilling over it. Window boxes were filled with a riot of colorful flowers, and containers lining the steps teemed with pink and white blooms.

Nicky bounced along the walkway to the front door, eager to get inside to see Queenie. When Viv opened the door, the cat was sitting there waiting, and she and the dog took off to the kitchen where Lin let them out into the fenced yard.

"Who'd ever guess that those two would be such fast friends," she said watching them fly into the yard and run around the trees chasing each other.

"They always make me smile." Viv took a pitcher of lemonade and iced tea from the refrigerator and poured it into two glasses. "Want to sit on the deck?" She carried a platter of hummus, tzatziki sauce, and pita bread and they sat down under the table umbrella to enjoy the snack.

"The sky looks threatening." Lin noticed dark clouds gathering in the western sky.

"Hopefully, it will just blow over."

"The door to the ell is unlatched." An addition to the old Cape house jutted off the back of the place that Sebastian and Emily had called their home. Viv used the space as a storage shed, and a few years ago, she and Lin found money, valuable artwork, gold coins, and jewelry in the ell that had been hidden there by their ancestors. The items had been gifts to Sebastian and Emily from people who had been accused of witchcraft or had experienced other forms of persecution. The couple had written in their diaries that they didn't ask for or want payment for the help they gave to people, but some insisted they take the gifts, and so, they hid the things in the ell, refusing to profit from the misfortune of others.

Early appraisals had estimated the stash was worth about half a million dollars, but the real value was much higher. Viv gave the horseshoe necklace to Lin, kept a few old maps, gave a few pieces of artwork to the Nantucket Historical Society, and then donated the rest to a museum in Boston.

"I don't need any more than what I have," Viv had said. "It wouldn't be right for a private citizen to own such valuable, historical items. They belong in a museum where people can enjoy seeing them. Our ancestors wouldn't profit from those things, and neither will I."

Anton, Libby, and Lin encouraged her to change her mind, but Viv wasn't having it.

Lin got up, went down the deck steps, and locked the ell door. When she returned to her chair, she smiled. "You know, I was thinking recently about the day we found the treasure in the shed. It was so unexpected and exciting." She reached up to touch her necklace.

"It would have remained hidden if you didn't decipher the anagram that led us to it." Viv sipped from her glass.

"I'm so grateful to have the necklace."

"And I'm happy I decided to keep a few old maps," Viv said.

Lin smiled. "Especially the one that's supposed to have belonged to the pirate La Buse." La Buse, a French pirate whose real name was Olivier Levasseur, lived from around 1690-1730 and supposedly hid a treasure worth over a billion dollars in today's money. It is said he also left behind a cryptogram providing clues to where the treasure was hidden.

"Well, sometimes I fantasize that we'll go on a treasure hunt someday. Imagine if we were the ones who found the treasure?"

"Unlikely," Lin shook her head.

"As unlikely as being able to see ghosts and bring them peace?"

Lin chuckled. "Yes, as unlikely as that."

"Then that means we'll find it." As Viv raised her glass of lemonade and iced tea and clinked it against Lin's, Nicky and Queenie dashed up the steps and onto the porch, and in two seconds a boom of thunder shook the house as large rain drops began to fall.

The women and the pets hurried into the house just as the wind kicked up.

Lin and Viv put the platter and the glasses in the dishwasher and then went into the living room to watch the pelting rain through the big picture window.

Nicky and Queenie jumped into an easy chair and stared out at the storm.

People caught in the torrential rain ran past the house trying to get where they wanted to go.

"This will clear out the humidity," Viv said. "It's been pretty uncomfortable lately." She turned around to see Lin standing in front of the framed maps hanging on one wall of the living room. "Lin?"

Lin looked over at her cousin.

"Why are you looking at the maps?" Viv asked.

"Because earlier, we were talking about finding the things Emily and Sebastian hid in the ell."

Viv walked to stand next to her. "Rumor has it that La Buse's treasure is buried somewhere in the Seychelles."

Lin's eyes roved over the map that supposedly had belonged to the pirate. "It isn't."

"What? What do you mean? Everything written about La Buse states that if there really is a treasure, then it's buried in the Seychelles."

Lin shrugged a shoulder without taking her eyes from the map. "Well, it isn't there. Treasure hunters are looking in the wrong place."

Viv put a hand on her hip. "How do you know?"

"Because ... I know."

Viv stared at her cousin. "Where is it then?"

Lin elbowed Viv and smiled. "That, I don't know."

"Try to figure it out before we get too old to go find it."

Letting out a sigh, Lin placed two fingers on the frame of La Buse's map. "Sometimes, everyone thinks things are one way, when in fact, they're something completely different."

Viv looked at her cousin with a blank expression. "Is that statement something from philosophy or is it relevant to our lives in some way?"

Lin didn't answer for a few seconds. "I think it has to do with the Main Street ghost."

Confused, Viv asked, "So, he isn't what we think?"

Lin scrunched up her face. "I don't know what I mean."

"That's what I like about you," Viv chuckled. "You always know exactly what's going on."

Nicky woofed and wagged his tail at Lin.

Lin and Viv both got texts at the same time from Libby. She and Anton were in town and were planning to have dinner down by the docks. She invited the cousins to join them.

"Let's go. Then we don't have to cook dinner," Lin suggested.

"And we won't have to clean up afterwards either. I'm in." Viv glanced out the window. "The rain's over. I can see some patches of blue sky."

"We'll be back after dinner," Lin told the cat and dog. "You two mind the house. We'll put your dinner out now before we leave."

Chatting as they went, the young women strolled down the brick sidewalks into town being careful to avoid the puddles left behind by the downpour. People were everywhere, looking in shop windows, heading to restaurants, pubs, or down to the docks. A ferry had just docked and the sidewalks were full of passengers pulling suitcases, pushing bicycles, and looking for taxis.

"Summer should be longer. I love tourist season." Lin smiled at the hustle and bustle.

Viv nudged Lin. "Isn't that April Blake over there?"

April was standing by a clothing boutique scrolling on her phone.

The cousins approached and called hello.

"Oh, hi." April smiled.

"How are you doing?" Viv asked with a concerned tone in her voice.

"I'm good. I'm sorry about the other night. I guess I overreacted."

"You didn't. Call us any time, day or night," Lin told her. "Did you go to the police? Did you show them the note?"

"I did." April frowned. "It isn't enough for them to do anything. The island is full of tourists and natives keeping them busy. There isn't anything in the note that gives the police a clue as to who the Mailman is. They said they'd go by my house now and then, but that's all they can do unless things get worse or I get an idea about who is leaving the notes."

Lin's shoulders drooped. "It's disappointing, but I understand. Did you show the letter to your parents?"

April hesitated. "I didn't. It will only upset them unnecessarily. There's nothing we can do."

"I think you should keep them informed." Lin encouraged the young woman to share what happened with her parents.

"It's better that they know," Viv assured April. "They need to be aware."

April looked reluctant.

"Have you been keeping an eye out for anyone who might be showing any unusual interest in you?"

"I do try to pay attention to that. I haven't noticed anything."

Viv said, "Well, keep your guard up. Is your friend still staying with you?"

"No, she only stayed that one night. I make sure all the windows and doors are locked when I'm in the apartment. And I keep my phone and pepper spray right beside me. I feel better when my days are normal. I can't live in fear all the time."

Lin agreed and then asked, "Could we get together some night? We could have dinner or something. I think it would be helpful for the three of us to talk about all of this."

"That would be nice. I don't know how much it will help. This mess has been going on for years and years, but … fresh eyes, and all that."

They made arrangements to meet, and then Lin and Viv headed to the restaurant to join Libby and Anton.

"It's going to be awfully hard to crack this case," Lin said as they approached the dockside food establishment.

Viv slipped her arm through her cousin's. "But not impossible."

Lin gave her a warm smile. "No, never impossible."

10

Lin and Viv joined Anton and Libby at their table by the window. It was dark outside and the lights reflected pools of shimmering gold on the water in the harbor. Anton and Libby were sipping cocktails when the cousins sat down.

"I thought it would be nice to have you come by," Libby said. "It's a pleasant place to chat, and we'd like to hear how the case is going. Well, the two cases, actually."

"I'm still researching the house and owners," Anton reported. "So far, I haven't found anything of note, but there has to be something. The *presence* in the house indicates that. Something made the ghost remain, and this isn't a case of not crossing over due to being happy in the house and not wanting to leave. The spirit is too agitated for that."

"I agree. We were at the historical museum earlier today. Felix produced a list of owners of the house. We tried to find some articles online, but so far, we're coming up empty," Lin told them.

The waiter brought drinks for Lin and Viv and a plate of appetizers.

Viv sipped. "We also went back to the Main Street house. The new owners were just leaving. They seem like nice people."

"I haven't met them," Libby said. "I don't know who they are."

"I don't know them either." Anton chose a chicken wing from the platter.

"They seem to spend most of the summer here," Lin explained. "Then they return to the mainland and come back for weekends every now and then in the off-seasons."

"What do they do for work?" Libby reached for her napkin and dabbed her lips.

"I don't know," Viv shrugged. "The topic hasn't come up."

"They still aren't concerned about the angry spirit?"

"No," Lin said. "They seem to think all the

changes with the house are the reason the ghost is agitated."

"Well, that is possible," Libby nodded. "But I would say not in this case."

"I agree. It's something more than restoration work and new owners that has the ghost so enraged and sad." Lin used the serving fork to bring some stuffed mushrooms to her plate. "I'm hopeful he'll communicate something to us soon. The last two times we were at the house, a piece of paper appeared on a desk and a pen hovered over it. I think he's trying his best to tell us something."

"This is fascinating." Anton sat straighter. "You still haven't seen him?"

"No," Viv shared. "He howls and yells and throws things across the room, but he stays hidden from us."

"He also causes knocking sounds on the walls and ringing phones," Lin added. "Today, we heard things being thrown and smashed, but when we went upstairs to see what was going on, there was nothing on the floors and no dents in the walls."

"That's good news." Libby set her drink down. "Then his purpose isn't to harm anyone. His behaviors are only to get your attention."

Salads arrived and they all dug in.

"Maybe he doesn't know how to communicate with us, and his inability to reach out successfully is frustrating him," Lin suggested.

"It all makes perfect sense." Anton added a bit more dressing to his salad. "And what about April Blake? What's going on with her?"

The cousins took turns reporting what happened the other night at April's house.

"So the pest is turning up the volume on his stalking." Libby looked disgusted.

"The wording of the note could be a veiled threat," Anton said, "but on the other hand, when he writes that April will be sorry, that could simply mean that her choices will make her unhappy, not that he'll do something to hurt her."

Lin stared at the man. "That's an interesting interpretation. Did we take it the wrong way?"

"Only time will tell," Anton said solemnly.

"And what about the police? The young woman showed them the note?" Libby asked.

"She did. The police will drive by her house on occasion, but there really isn't anything else they can do," Viv told them. "We're going to meet April for dinner soon. That will give us a chance to ask a bunch of questions about the Mailman."

"We need a lot more information if we're going to come up with some suspects," Lin added.

"Unless the man is caught in the act or gets captured on a security camera, I think it will be very difficult to solve," Libby admitted. "Do what you can, but don't berate yourselves if nothing comes of your efforts."

The meals were served, and everyone was pleased with their orders.

"I've been thinking about the Main Street house," Lin shared. "There has to be someone besides the couple who owned the house who has heard of something happening there. The couple might have shared information about an unfortunate incident from the past that had been passed down over the generations. Maybe a friend? Maybe someone who worked for them?"

"Let me ask around," Libby said. "My contacts might know who the couple socialized with. Or perhaps, an associate of mine used the same landscaper or housekeeper. I'll let you know if I discover anything."

After dinner, Libby and Anton were meeting a friend on his boat for a drink, and Lin and Viv decided to head home. Lin needed to pick up Nicky and tomorrow, they both had early days at work.

The town was still bustling. The sidewalks were crowded, there were lines of people at some of the pubs, and street musicians played on a few corners giving the place a festive atmosphere.

"I'd love to listen to some music at one of the pubs." Viv peeked inside one of her favorite nightspots as they walked past.

"I'll go in with you, if you want." Lin eyed her cousin. "As long as you don't stay until closing."

"It's tempting, but we've had long days and tomorrow promises to be another long one. Let's just head back to the house and call it a night."

Lin yawned. "I'm glad that was your answer. If we went to a pub, I'd probably fall asleep on the table."

"And then I'd have to carry you home."

As they walked up Main Street, the crowds thinned until there were only one or two people passing by. The puddles from the earlier rainstorm had dried up and stars twinkled overhead.

Viv talked about ordering new books for her shop, hiring a couple more staff members, and preparing the store for the upcoming Labor Day sale.

"It will be Christmastime before you know it and then there'll be the Stroll with the tourists coming in for the big weekend of activities."

"It's still August, you know," Lin reminded her cousin.

"But I have to plan sales and make sure I have enough staff for these events. The stroll is four months away. I have to be ready."

"I love the Christmas Stroll. The beautiful decorations, the parade, all the people, it's all so great."

"We should do some serious planning about the winter vacation we want to take," Viv said. "We talk about it every year, and then we get too busy and it's too late. The guys don't care where we go, but it has to be warm and there has to be an ocean. The rest is up to us."

"What about someplace in the Caribbean?"

"I'd like that. It would be relaxing and laid-back."

When Lin got quiet as they made their way to Viv's neighborhood, Viv noticed.

"Are you trying to figure out where La Buse's pirate treasure is hidden? It must be buried at a tropical island. We can swim and sun, and in our free time go hunting for treasure," Viv joked. "Lin? Come back to Earth. You're in never-never land."

Lin moved her eyes from side to side. She whispered, "I feel someone nearby."

As a chill ran down Viv's back, she kept her voice soft. "What does that mean exactly?"

"I'm not sure. Don't be obvious about it, but do you notice anyone lurking anywhere?"

"Are we in danger?" Viv put her arm through her cousin's and pulled her close.

"No. I don't know. Probably not. Just stay aware."

Viv groaned. "That wasn't your best answer."

"Do you hear footsteps?"

Viv spun her head around to see if anyone was following them.

"That wasn't obvious at all," Lin rolled her eyes. "Now, he'll know we're on to him."

"Good, then maybe he'll go away." Viv's heart began to race. "Wait. Do you think it's the Mailman? He could have seen us with April the other night at her house. Maybe he wants to see where we're going."

"Let's loop around and head back into town," Lin suggested.

The women picked up the pace and made a circle to go back to the main streets of Nantucket town, and then decided to go to the docks and get John from his boat so he could walk them home.

Lin let out a long breath. "Sorry. I was probably imagining things."

"You don't imagine things and I never doubt your sixth sense," Viv told her. "Someone was watching us. I know it."

11

While Nicky sniffed around the yard, Lin and Leonard worked in one of their client's extensive gardens weeding, removing dead blooms, replacing flowers that were past their prime, and edging. They'd already mowed the lawn and trimmed some bushes.

Lin pulled her sweaty t-shirt away from her body and flapped the end to attempt to dry it a little. "Too bad the humidity is back."

"Too bad these clients don't have a pool we can jump in." Leonard wiped his brow.

Lin chuckled. "We'll have to speak to them about that. Let's sit in the shade for a few minutes. I'm melting."

When they sat down under a big tree and sipped

from their water bottles, the dog came over and plopped down next to them. Lin offered him some water, but he wasn't interested.

Leonard asked about the Main Street ghost. "Has he written anything yet with that pen and paper?"

"Not yet." Lin updated him on the spirit's antics. "If we could just pinpoint when he died, we'd have a better idea who he was and why he doesn't cross over."

"It's a shame the previous owners didn't have family. They might have been able to give you some information." Leonard took another long drink from his bottle. "Heather's been worried about April Blake. I told her I didn't think there was any news."

"There really isn't. The new note from the other night is the only thing that's happened. No news is good news. Viv and I are going to meet April and her older sister Julie for dinner. Julie is in her last year of medical school. She was eighteen when the notes started. We'll pick their brains and see if anyone they knew back then could be a suspect."

"It could be someone they didn't know well. A secret admirer, maybe," Leonard offered.

"The notes always have been more frequent in the summer, but the sisters still received them in the off-seasons so it has to be someone who either lives on-island or someone who visits here all year round."

"And there was a time when the notes stopped, or they became way less frequent, right?"

"Yes, but I don't recall when that happened. I'll bring it up with the sisters when we get together."

"Let's finish up here. We have to get to that meeting with the possible new client soon." Leonard pushed himself up from the grass. "This garden bed is going to need a little more mulch. Would you make a note on your phone so we bring some next time?"

Lin tapped at her phone while following Leonard back to the garden beds.

In less than an hour, they had finished up and were ready to go see the new client.

"Why don't you and the cur ride with me and we'll pick up your truck on the way back?"

"Fine with me, but I don't think Nicky appreciates being called a cur." Lin opened the truck door and the dog jumped in, wagging his stump of a tail.

"He doesn't mind. He knows it's a term of endearment." Leonard fired up the engine and they were off to the Shawkemo neighborhood of the island. Located on the northern coastline, Shawkemo was home to some of the most luxurious houses on the island. Many were either on the inner harbor or had panoramic views of it.

"So this guy we're going to see is Mr. Money Pants, right?" Lin had the window down and was enjoying the breeze on her face.

"That's right." Leonard glanced at Lin. "He's also known as Thomas Linton-Campbell."

With a chuckle, Lin said, "I know. I wasn't really going to call him Mr. Money Pants. I looked up the property. His place is huge. There's the main house, a guest cottage about four times the size of my house, a staff house, garages, a pool and pool house, and a greenhouse. He has ten full-time staff. The buildings are enclosed by a walled English garden and orchard. There are fifty acres of conservation land abutting his land. There are acres of gardens and walking trails around the property."

"So you don't know anything about the place, I guess." Leonard turned the steering wheel to turn onto a smaller road.

"Nothing at all." Lin grinned.

"Did you look up the owner?"

"Nah. I only care about the property. He wants us to design a new garden for him, but is that all? He doesn't expect us to take over the care of the grounds, does he?"

"No, he has staff for that. He heard we were good. He wants to hear what we have to say about the new gardens. Heather told him about our business, and it seems Mr. Linton-Campbell had heard of us."

"How does Heather know him?"

"She did some legal work for him."

"Huh. I would have thought he'd only want a high-powered attorney from New York City handling his affairs."

"It was something he wanted done quickly and Heather was recommended to him by a Nantucket friend." Leonard pulled into a long, winding driveway and passed by some open green fields, mature trees, and beautifully laid-out gardens.

"Is this guy sure he wants to talk to *us*?"

"We have plenty of wealthy clients, Coffin."

When the house came into view, Lin gasped. "Whoa, look at this. It's incredible."

An enormous, sprawling two-story mansion, covered in traditional Nantucket weathered shingles, stood before them. The driveway was paved with bricks, but the parking pad was covered in crushed white shells. The landscaping around the house and garages was impeccable.

The landscapers and the dog emerged from the

truck and before they'd taken ten steps, a man came out of the house and made his way down to them.

"Hello. You must be Leonard Reed and Lin Coffin. You found the place with no trouble?"

"We did, thanks," Leonard nodded.

"Mr. Linton-Campbell is in the rear yard. I'll take you to him."

Lin spoke up. "If Mr. Linton-Campbell would prefer, I can have my dog wait here by the truck. He's very well-trained and well-behaved."

"Not at all. Mr. Linton-Campbell loves dogs. He'll be happy to see him. If you'll follow me." The man led the way along stone walkways through rose gardens and wildflower gardens, around the house to the rear of the property.

A man in his early-sixties stood staring at the lawns, but turned when he heard footsteps.

"Hello, there," he called. "Welcome."

Linton-Campbell was tall and fit-looking with salt and pepper hair and light blue eyes. He was dressed in chinos, deck shoes, and a blue shirt with the sleeves rolled up. "Oh, wonderful. You brought a dog with you." Before shaking hands with Leonard and Lin, he knelt down to pet Nicky.

"What's his name?" The man ran his hand over the soft fur and scratched the dog behind his ears.

"Nicky. He's a rescue dog."

"A fine animal. He seems to have a sweet temperament."

"He does, indeed. He's a good friend to me," Lin said.

Linton-Campbell stood. "Man's ... and woman's best friend. I've found that to be true over the years. My dogs have truly been some of my dearest friends."

Lin liked the man immediately.

"You have a beautiful home," Lin told him.

"I'm a very lucky person. I never take any of it for granted. I thank the heavens every day for my good fortune. It is beyond anything I ever dreamed of. I'm a believer that dreams can come true."

"You have family?" Lin asked.

"Oh, yes. My greatest blessing. My wife, Gemma, and I have been together for over forty years. We married when we were twenty. We have five children, fifteen grandchildren, and two great-grandchildren." The man beamed.

"A life well-lived," Leonard told him. "I never had any children. My wife died young. My greatest regret was losing her and not having children together."

"I'm so very sorry," Linton-Campbell said with sympathy in his tone.

Leonard nodded at Lin. "But this young woman has blessed my life with her friendship ... for which I'm forever grateful. She's like the daughter I never had."

Lin had to blink back a couple of tears. She was surprised to hear her friend's words. Leonard never spoke so openly with someone he'd just met.

"Business partners *and* dear friends." Linton-Campbell looked pleased to hear it. "Well, let me show you what I'd like done with the yard, then I'll give you a tour of the grounds, if you have the time. Oh, where are my manners? Would you like something to drink before we chat about the landscaping?"

"No, thank you."

"And please, call me Thomas." He walked Lin and Leonard to a wide expanse of lawn. "I just don't think having so much lawn is a good thing. My wife and I would like to have more wildflower gardens here. They'd provide cover and food for some of the wildlife." He talked about the wildflowers he'd like planted.

"We'd like to have things native to the island. I would also like to have some blueberry bushes and strawberry plants here for the wildlife."

As they walked around, Lin wrote notes on her

phone and took photographs of the area for later
reference, and when they were done, Thomas gave
them a tour of the magnificent gardens.

"Gemma and I are hosting an end-of-summer
party here. We'll send you invitations. Please join us.
Bring your husband, and some of your friends. We'd
love to have you come. I know it's a last minute invi-
tation, so don't feel obligated should you have other
plans." He gestured to the back of the property.
"There are walking trails down this way. I'd like to
take you down to the inner harbor. It's quite lovely, if
you'd like to see it."

"We'd love to."

Thomas gave them a history of the land and the
house. "I had a friend design the place after we
purchased the land. The land was originally owned
by the Bean family. A very early family on the
island."

Lin's eyes widened.

"But being a Coffin, you must know a good deal
about the early settlers," Thomas said to Lin.

"The Bean family owned the land?"

"They did, well, generations ago. Gemma is a
very distant member of the Bean family so we were
delighted to buy this piece of property."

"My husband is restoring a house on Main Street

that was owned by the Beans for decades, centuries, really," Lin told him.

"I know the house. Nicholas and Catherine Whittaker owned it. Catherine was a direct descendant of the Bean family," Thomas explained. "Someone new has recently purchased it. Do you know their names?"

"Michael and Eileen Salem," Lin reported.

Thomas tapped at his chin. "I've met them a few times. Gemma and Eileen are members of the garden club."

"They seem like nice people."

The trail ended with a spectacular view of the inner harbor. A wooden pier stretched out into the water. Four Adirondack chairs were placed at the end of the dock.

"Shall we walk out?" Thomas led the way along the long pier. "My wife and I like to come down here in the evenings and sit with mugs of tea. It's so very peaceful."

Nicky leaned over to watch fish swimming in the quiet water.

"There's always been a trail leading to the harbor here," Thomas told them. "I like to imagine some of the Beans fishing or walking along the shore hundreds of years ago."

When Lin looked down into the water from the end of the dock, a strange feeling washed over her and she felt dizzy for a few seconds. A sense of terrible dread flowed through her veins and made her step back.

"Well, it's getting late," she managed to say. "We should really be going."

Leonard gave his partner a strange look.

All Lin wanted was to get out of there as fast as she could.

12

The next evening while walking into town to meet April Blake and her sister, Lin told Viv about the visit to Thomas Linton-Campbell's estate.

"And then when we were down by the water, I walked out onto the small wooden dock they have and a terrible rush of anxiety raced through me. I couldn't shake it. It got worse and worse. I had to get out of there. Leonard thought I'd lost my mind."

Viv looked at her cousin with worry. "What do you think it was about?"

"I don't know for sure, but I think it's tied to the Main Street ghost or to the Blake sisters' notes from the Mailman."

"Really? In what way?"

"It's a mystery to me. It was such an awful feeling. It was dread, and anxiety, and fear all rolled up into a big, pulsing mess. I'm starting to sweat just thinking about it."

"How will you figure out what it means?" Viv asked.

"I don't know if I'll be able to figure it out. I could ask April if she or her sisters have some link to the inner harbor, but that will definitely get me some oddball looks."

"Ask anyway. It could be an important clue. What about the ghost? Will you ask him about the area near the harbor?"

"I may as well. We've got nothing else to go on."

They entered the pub and spotted April sitting at a table with a woman who looked just like her. Taking seats in the booth, the young women shared introductions.

"Nice to meet you both." Twenty-six-year old Julie Blake had the same strawberry blond hair as her sister, but hers just touched her shoulders, and the lovely green eyes appeared to be a sibling trait. "It's so nice of you to help out with the family problem."

"We're glad to lend a hand," Lin said. "We hope it can lead to something fruitful."

The four women ordered meals and then went

on chatting.

"Just to get the facts straight," Viv began, "this all started when you were about eighteen?"

"That's right." Recalling the beginning of the Mailman's antics, Julie's face took on a look of concern. "I was the one who got the mail that day. It was written to me. At first, I was flattered to think I had a secret admirer."

"The feeling of flattery disappeared real fast," April told them.

"That's for sure. It all got really weird, really fast. A note came at least once a week, sometimes more. It was clear the person knew a lot about me, where I spent my time, who I spent my time with. We called the police, but there wasn't anything they could do. For a while, I stopped doing things. I just went to school and stayed close to our house. Then I got annoyed and decided I wasn't going to allow some weirdo to control my life so I returned to my activities."

"Right before Julie's high school graduation," April said, "the notes started to be addressed to the twins, Molly and Mallory, and sometimes to me, but not very often. After about a year of that, the notes always had all three of our names on them. He must have been preparing for Molly and Mallory to go off to college so he included me in the notes. It was the same crazy stuff, mentioning where he saw us, what we were doing, who we were with. It's so unnerving to think that someone is watching you. It makes my skin crawl."

"Was the content of the notes usually the same every time?" Viv questioned.

April and Julie looked at each other. "Yeah, just about."

"Was there ever anything threatening in them?" Lin looked from one sister to the other.

"Not really," Julie replied. "Nothing overt. But the notes *felt* like threats."

"We're going to toss out some ideas," Lin told them. "What about a former boyfriend? Was there someone any of you dated who might have resorted to writing the notes? Just think about it for a minute. Or was there someone interested in one of you, but who got rejected?"

"There was a guy I dated late in my senior year," Julie thought back. "Jason Price." She turned to her sister who nodded. "It wasn't the right match for me. He just wasn't my type. He was way too *into* me. He was too solicitous. He was too fawning. It made me so uncomfortable. I hated to do it, but I stopped seeing him after three dates."

"Does he still live on-island?" Lin asked.

"He does," April reported. "He does interior painting. I think he lives over by Cisco Beach."

"I haven't seen him in a long time," Julie said. "I wasn't sure he was still living on Nantucket."

"How about you and the twins?" Lin looked at April. "Did anyone want to date you, but was rebuffed? Anyone with a crush on any of you?"

"I don't think so," April said. "I can't remember anyone like that."

"What about a teacher or a coach?" Viv brought up the people at the school. "Was anyone a little too friendly? Maybe someone who was a little too controlling?"

"My coaches were all nice," Julie said. "I was on the track team and the basketball team. I wouldn't suspect any of the people connected to my sports."

Lin leaned forward. "Since the notes started coming to you, Julie, I think we should focus on your time on the island. You were probably the initial attraction."

"I've thought about that many times. I wonder and wonder what I did to start this." Julie pushed a strand of hair from her face.

"You didn't do anything," Lin assured her. "This is all the perpetrator's doing."

"Can you recall a teacher or a coach who paid a little too much attention to you?" Viv attempted to jog the young woman's memory. "Or a janitor or someone who worked in the school office?"

Julie shook her head. "Nothing stands out."

"Okay. We're going to try and jog your memory," Lin said. "What about at your parents' restaurant? You must have worked there from time to time?"

"I did. We all did."

"Thinking back, does a customer or a co-worker stand out as someone who seemed interested in you?"

Julie slumped against the booth. "I'm no help at all. I never noticed anyone who seemed too interested in me. I wish I could go back in time and interact with people for a week. I bet I'd have a better idea who it was."

"If only." Lin nodded.

"Your family attended church?" Viv questioned.

Both sisters nodded.

"How about a church-goer? The organist? A deacon? Did anyone seem to want to talk to you a lot? Did anyone seem to keep their eye on you? Did someone seem overly friendly toward you?"

Julie tilted her head to the side. "Well, the organist heard me sing at a school concert and then kept badgering me to join the choir and be a soloist at church. I didn't want to take on the commitment, so I always said no."

Lin and Viv perked up.

"Who was the organist?" Lin inquired.

"Bill Barre," Julie said.

"He still plays the organ at the church," April told them.

"How old is he would you guess?"

"I'd say about forty?" April shrugged.

"I'd guess the same," Julie nodded.

"Okay, what about a neighbor?" Viv asked.

"Everyone in our neighborhood seems nice," Julie reported.

"Are all the houses in the neighborhood owned by fulltime residents?"

"No, some houses are used mainly in the summer. A couple of houses are rented out to tourists in the summers," April explained. "But most places are owned by fulltime people."

"Let's talk about the frequency of the notes," Lin suggested. "The summer has always been the busiest time for the notes to arrive, right?"

"That's right," April said.

"But they still show up in the off-seasons?"

"Yeah, but there isn't a pattern to when they get

delivered. It all seems pretty random."

Lin felt like they'd gotten at least two leads from the discussion and planned to speak with the two people Julie talked about, the home painter Jason Price, who she dated in high school only three times, and the organist at the church Bill Barre. It wasn't much, but one thing could lead to another so she was hopeful.

The young women ate their meals and talked about other things besides the Mailman and his stalking of the Blake sisters.

When they were done and were walking past the bar on their way to the exit, someone called Julie's name, and they all turned to see who it was.

A tall, fit, dark-haired nicely-dressed young man in his mid to late twenties, stood smiling at Julie.

"Hey, Julie. You're home. Nice to see you."

"You, too. You know my sister. And these are two friends, Lin and Viv." Julie smiled back at the man. "How are you doing?

"Doing well. Running my shop, expanding the product line. How long will you be on-island?"

"Not long. A few days. I have to get back to the hospital. I'm lucky I got a few days off."

"You're in Boston?"

"Yeah, doing hours in different departments. It

can be intense."

"Maybe we can meet for a drink before you go back?"

"That would be nice."

They exchanged numbers and the man said, "I'll give you a call."

The four women continued on their way out of the pub.

"Who was that?" Lin asked.

"Peter Norton. We went to high school together," Julie told them.

"Did you date?" asked Viv.

"We didn't."

"But you wanted to," April reminded her sister. "And Peter was always into you."

"We were never single at the same time," Julie explained. "It just never worked out."

"He lives here?"

Julie nodded. "He has a café and specialty food shop in Madaket, Pete's Provisions. I hear he's doing really well."

The women chatted as they walked and then parted ways. Lin and Viv continued up Main Street.

"Let me guess," Viv eyed her cousin. "Peter Norton is on your list of people to talk to."

"You bet he is."

13

It was late afternoon when Lin and Nicky stopped by Viv's bookstore. Lin needed an iced coffee and a sweet to give her a pick-me-up after working since 7am in the hot sun.

Viv was at the beverage counter in the back of the shop and started the iced drink before Lin even got close.

"You saw me coming?"

"I did. She set the beverage in front of her cousin. "Want something to eat?"

Lin took a look at the glass pastry display. "Everything looks good. What do I want?" She bent to get a better look into the case. "I'll take a chocolate chip banana muffin."

"Are you going to sit?"

"No, I'll take it with me. Yesterday, Jeff told Michael and Eileen Salem that I was a landscaper and they called me in the evening to ask if I could come by and look at their yard. They want me and Leonard to do some work for them. I'm going to swing by and see what they have in mind. I'm not sure we can fit it in, unless we hire another crew."

"Are you going to stop inside while you're there?" Viv wiped down the counter.

"I don't think I will. If the guys are working, then there won't be any use going inside. I wouldn't be able to talk to the ghost."

"We should go back by ourselves pretty soon," Viv suggested.

"We should. I'll ask Jeff what this week's work schedule looks like and we can work around that."

"Okay. You'll come by later and pick me up?"

"Yeah. I'll text you when I'm on my way."

"I haven't been to Pete's Provisions in months. I had no idea who owned the place. Hope we get some information from him."

"Me, too. I'm glad we ran into him with Julie and April the other night. I'll see you in a couple of hours." Lin picked up her iced coffee and the bag with her muffin in it, turned, called Nicky, and then they were off to the truck.

Michael and Eileen Salem were in the front yard of the Main Street house when Lin pulled the truck alongside the curb. They came over as she and the dog were getting out.

"Afternoon," Michael called.

"We're so glad you had time today to take a look at the yard," Eileen smiled.

"I had some time so it worked out. How are things?"

"Everything's fine," Michael said.

Lin sensed some tension between him and his wife.

"Are you interested in having the front and rear yards done?" Lin asked as they walked closer to the house.

"As you can see," Michael said, "it's all been quite neglected for some time."

"We'd love to have hydrangeas around the front and sides of the house," Eileen pointed to where she thought they should go. "We'd also like some flower beds, here and here."

Lin used her phone to take some notes and photograph the yard.

"And the lawn's a mess." Michael frowned. "Would you pull it all up and start from scratch?"

"I don't think that would be necessary. I think

overseeding, putting down some lime, giving it some organic fertilizer, and it would be rejuvenated. It would take four to eight months to get it where you want it, but it would be efficient and economical."

Nicky sniffed along the old beds full of weeds.

As they walked around to the back of the home, Eileen asked, "Are you making any headway with the ... the *resident* who comes with the house?"

"Some. These things can take a bit of time."

Eileen let out a sigh. "Every time we go inside, it seems worse."

"Oh, come on, Eileen." Michael rolled his eyes.

Lin turned to look at the woman. "How so?"

"Now, as soon as we step inside, it starts to knock and moan and a phone starts ringing. It sounds like things are being tossed across the room upstairs, but when we go up there, there's nothing on the floor and no damage. It's really getting on my nerves. The spirit who lived in our other house was nothing like this."

"Lin will sort it out," Michael said. "We have months before the house will be completed and we can move in. It will be fine. You need to stop worrying about it."

Eileen ignored her husband. "When the restoration is complete, if the ghost is still carrying on like it does, then I'd like to put the house on the market at that time."

"That's understandable," Lin agreed. "Wait and see how things go."

"We're sinking a ton of money into this place," Michael protested.

Eileen snapped, "And we'll make a handsome profit if we do decide to sell."

To ease the tension, Lin said, "Tell me what you're thinking for the rear yard."

Eileen crossed her arms over her chest.

Michael said, "We'd like gardens on this side, and on the other side, we'd like to put in a patio and a pergola and maybe have some flowering bushes around it. The lawn is shot, so maybe you could do the same things here that you plan to do with the front lawn. We want to keep that section near the fence all lawn for now. Maybe in the future, we can put in a plunge pool."

"Well, good. I think I have what I need. I'll talk to my partner and we'll look at our fall schedule. I can't promise we can take this on. We're pretty busy, but we'll discuss and I'll get back to you. If we can do it, we'll need to meet again to get some more details. I'll let you know in about a week."

As the Salems were walking out to the car, Jeff

came out of the house and Nicky darted to greet him.

"Hey, Nick." Jeff bent to pat the happy dog, and then stood and gave Lin a kiss. "I saw the Salems leaving so I came out to see how it went."

"It went well. I just don't know if we can squeeze them in. I'll talk it over with Leonard." Lin told her husband that the couple had been arguing about the ghost.

"The ghost is quiet when we're working. Some things get moved around or some tools go missing for a few minutes, but overall, he isn't causing any trouble. The other guys don't even notice. I did come by one day to get a few power tools for another job, and the Salems were here. The ghost was putting on quite a show."

"What was he doing?"

"It didn't seem like grief or sadness. It sounded like anger. There was loud pounding on the walls, unintelligible shouting, phones ringing, doors slamming over and over again. I get why Eileen wouldn't want to live here. I wouldn't want to either."

"I'm hoping that by the time the restoration is complete, the ghost will either have calmed down or will have crossed over."

"I hope you're right because it sounds furious

about something right now." Jeff glanced at the house. "Maybe he doesn't like the Salems?"

"It could be that he's upset by the changes. The former owners died, and now there are new people in the house. Not to mention the construction going on."

"Yeah, it's a lot." Jeff hugged his wife. "I'd better get back to work. I'll see you at home this evening. I'll cook." He scratched Nicky behind the ears. "Want Nick to stay here with me while you and Viv go to Pete's Provisions for your meeting?"

"I think he'd like that."

The couple kissed, and Jeff and the dog went inside the house.

Lin was on the sidewalk about to go around the truck to the driver's side when a car pulled up behind it and a man called to her. She turned to see an expensive Mercedes parking near her truck.

"Hello, Lin." Thomas Linton-Campbell got out and greeted her on the sidewalk. "I thought it was you. Is this the house where your husband is working? This is the home the Salems purchased?"

Lin nodded. "Nice to see you. The Salems just left. I met with them about doing some landscaping."

"Where's that great dog of yours?"

Lin laughed. "He's inside helping with the restoration."

Thomas chuckled. He gestured to the car and walked to the passenger side where he opened the door. An older man who looked to be in his early nineties sat staring forward.

"This is my father-in-law Matthew Bean. I'm taking him to a doctor's appointment. We're early so I thought I'd stop and say hello."

"Hello, Mr. Bean," Lin spoke to the man.

Thomas kept his voice low. "Matthew is dealing with dementia. He rarely speaks and when he does, it's just one word."

Lin nodded. "I see."

"My wife and I are looking forward to the landscaping you and Leonard will do at our house. We've seen your work around the island and it's second to none. You left a bit abruptly the other afternoon. Was everything all right?"

"Oh, yes, everything was fine. I apologize for my hasty retreat. I was coming down with a migraine," Lin fibbed. "I don't get them often, but when I do, they can be pretty severe. I wanted to get home before it kicked in."

"I've had three migraines in my life and that was three too many."

Matthew shifted in his seat and stared at the house.

"Has your father-in-law been a visitor here? He seems to recognize the home."

"I don't know. It's possible. It's also possible that he's confusing it with some other house."

Matthew's face brightened and he gestured toward the white Colonial. "Yes, yes."

Lin glanced at the house to see if one of the workers had stepped outside and had caught Matthew's attention, but no one had come out.

"Yes. Yes." Matthew's eyes were locked on the house.

"We'd better get going to the appointment," Thomas said. "I hope you and Leonard and your partners can come to the garden party. Bring some friends, if you like. We'll be having about a hundred people. Appetizers, drinks, desserts. And there will be music and dancing. Please join us." Thomas hurried around the Mercedes to get into the driver's seat.

Leaning a bit to see out of the open car window, Matthew's eyes were pinned on one of the house's second floor windows, and when Lin followed his gaze, she saw shimmering atoms behind the glass.

"Yes," the man said again.

Lin looked at the old man and he nodded to her. He pointed at the window. "Yes."

He sees the ghost.

She nodded to Matthew. "Yes," she said softly. "Yes."

14

Lin and Viv drove out to Madaket to speak with Peter Norton, a friend of Julie Blake, and on the way, Lin told her cousin how Thomas Linton-Campbell's father-in-law could see the ghost in one of the second floor windows of the Main Street house.

"Could you see the ghost?"

"I could see shimmering atoms, but they weren't formed." Lin maneuvered the truck along the winding road.

"Why could the father-in-law see the ghost and you couldn't?" Viv's expression showed one of confusion.

"I'm not sure. Maybe because he's closer to the other side than I am?"

"Oh, I hadn't thought of that." Viv watched the scenery go by as they made their way to the other side of the island.

"I'd like to go to the house tonight and see if the ghost will show himself. Want to come?"

"Sure, I'll go with you. Maybe he'll even write you a message with that pen he's always holding in the air. It's about time he helped you with some information."

"You can tell him that when we go there tonight," Lin smiled.

"First, I'll see what sort of mood he's in. I don't feel like getting a candlestick thrown at my head."

The road to Madaket was a picturesque ride past woods, meadow, and marshes. The bike path wove through the woods parallel to the street and Viv and Lin saw lots of cyclists, runners, and walkers taking advantage of the pleasant off-road byway.

"We need to go biking someday. Maybe on the weekend," Viv suggested. "We could pack lunch and take our swimsuits."

"Sounds good to me." Lin adjusted her sunglasses. "Have you thought about going to the Linton-Campbell's garden party?"

"Oh, yeah, I forgot to tell you I talked to John

about it. He's eager to go. He thinks it will be a good place to network and make connections for his real estate business. So we'd like to go with you. I think it will be fun."

"Great. I was hoping you'd come. Leonard and Heather are planning to go, too. I haven't met Mrs. Linton-Campbell, but Thomas is really friendly and nice."

"I have to pick out my outfit," Viv said. "Or, maybe, I'll get a new dress."

Madaket was located at the western end of the island and was known for its beautiful sunsets, soft sand beach, and sometimes, high surf. It had been home to Mildred Carpenter Jewett, fondly nick-named Madaket Millie, a Nantucket native who spent many years as a volunteer for the United States Coast Guard. In 1947, Millie noticed a steamer ship run aground off the coast. She was credited with saving the ship and crew by contacting the Coast Guard and organizing a rescue mission. The woman also served as a defense specialist during World War II watching the coast for signs of German submarines.

Not far from the beach, Lin turned the truck into a small lot next to Pete's Provisions, a gray-shingled cottage that housed a café and a specialty food shop with a brick patio right off the side entrance where there were plenty of tables for outdoor seating.

Inside, the place was cozy and bright with big windows bringing in lots of natural light. One side held the café and on the left were aisles and tables featuring locally made breads, jams, jellies, pastries, chocolate, artisan cheeses and coffees, specialty teas, farm-fresh vegetables, oils, sauces, honey, and many other delights.

A tall, dark-haired man approached with a wide smile. "Lin. Viv. Nice to see you. How about something to drink? We can take them outside and sit in the shade."

The cousins shook hands with Peter Norton.

"Thanks for meeting with us," Lin told him as they walked over to the counter to order drinks. Lin choose a vanilla smoothy and Viv tried an iced herbal tea.

Once outside, Peter chose a table off to the side for privacy, and the three of them sat down in comfortable outdoor chairs.

"Your place is great." Lin sipped her smoothy through a straw. "This is delicious."

"Glad you like it," Peter said.

"Mine, too. The tea is so light and flavorful."

"How long have you owned the shop?"

"About four years. I studied business in college. I always wanted to run my own store and I did a lot of brainstorming about what sort of place I'd like to open. There was a need for a niche food store and café so I decided to fill that need. This house came on the market and my mom and dad helped me by buying it. I'm paying them back over time. Dad and I did most of the renovations to turn it into a shop. Then I got financing to stock the place, hire employees, and we were in business. It's gone better than I could have imagined."

"We run small businesses, too," Viv told him. "We're always happy to hear about someone else's success."

"Thanks," Pete nodded. "So you want to talk about the stalker who's been bothering the Blakes."

"We have some research and interviewing experience. We've been able to provide some details and information that helped solve some cases." Lin stretched the truth a little, and left out the parts about helping ghosts.

"You knew Julie when you were in high school," Viv said. "That's when the unusual notes started showing up, in her senior year. We wanted to pick your brain."

"Good. Sure. When you called about meeting up, I thought for a second that you might suspect me."

"We don't have any suspects at all." Lin took another sip of her smoothy. "The notes have been arriving for so many years and no one has been caught. It's a difficult case. The person has to be caught in the act, and so far, he hasn't slipped up. We guess he's quite clever, quite smart, and careful. He has to be ... in order to have kept his identity a secret for so long."

Peter ran his hand through his dark hair. "It's kind of amazing that this has gone on for so long. What sort of satisfaction could it bring the perpetrator? I can understand an initial thrill, but really? All this time? Eight years? Or is it nine?"

Lin agreed, and then explained. "It's most likely issues of power and control. The perp knows he frightens the entire family with his notes. It throws them off-balance, puts them on edge. He gets a rush from making people keep looking over their shoulders. And he knows law enforcement can't do much about it so it's also a feeling of power over the police."

"I've never really given this much thought." Peter looked down at the wooden tabletop. "When I first heard about it, I thought it was some guy having a little fun bothering Julie and her sisters. It never occurred to me how it mentally affects the family. Who knows if or when the person might escalate? There must be strong feelings of violation, fears of getting attacked. It's really awful. And for it to continue for years? It has to be traumatizing."

"I'm sure it is," Lin told him. "Some people brush it off. 'Oh, it's just some notes. Ignore it,' they say. But it's psychological warfare. It's very damaging to the victims."

"How can I help?"

"Thinking back on senior year," Viv said, "does anyone stand out as having too strong an interest in Julie?"

"Most people thought Julie was great. She's smart, pretty, athletic. She was always nice to everyone, helpful, considerate. I think lots of people were attracted to her. Sure, guys wanted to date her, but mostly, people wanted to be friends with her, to hang out with her. She has a very magnetic personality, and really positive energy. People are drawn to her. That's what must have caught the perp's eye." Peter smiled shyly. "It's certainly what caught mine."

Viv asked, "Did you ever date Julie?"

Peter shook his head.

"Did you ever ask her out?"

"No, I didn't. One of us was always dating someone else when the other one was single. Then we went off to college. I came back to Nantucket, but Julie went on to medical school. We never seem to be in the right place, at the right time." Peter looked off in the direction of the sea. "So back to your question about someone who paid Julie more interest than one would expect. I don't know. I was a teenaged boy. I didn't pay much attention to things like that. I was wrapped up in my own life, my own friends. If I were to go back in time, I'd sure be paying attention to things like that."

"Did anyone back then seem a little ... I don't know ... off?" Viv questioned.

"There was a guy Julie dated a couple of times. He seemed infatuated with her. He was always quiet, unassuming. Jason Price. He was like a lap dog around her. He's still on the island. He has a painting business. I bumped into him at a pub a few times. He's got a lot more confidence now that he's matured. He's still quiet, but we had good talks when we saw each other at the pub. I don't think it's him who's sending the notes. Maybe when he was a high school kid, he'd drop a love note in someone's mailbox, but not now, and not for so many years. No way. It can't be him."

"Anyone else pop into your mind?" Lin asked.

Peter shrugged and lifted his hands in a helpless gesture. "I just don't know. No one stands out to me. It's been so long since we were in high school. I don't have a clue who could be doing this to the Blakes."

15

It was early evening when Lin and Viv returned to the Main Street house and entered the foyer. As soon as they switched on the lights, footsteps could be heard pacing around in the upstairs bedroom.

"Hello," Lin called. "It's me and Viv back again."

The pacing grew heavier and quicker like someone was hurrying back and forth across the room.

"Should we go up?" Viv asked.

Lin gave her a look of surprise. "You're getting brave."

With a shrug, she said, "Well, he hasn't hurt us yet. *Yet* being the important word."

Lin led the way upstairs and as soon as they

entered the large bedroom, she glanced over at the desk.

"A friend of mine stopped by to chat with me recently when I was standing in front of the house," she said to the ghost. "His father-in-law was with him. The older man sat in the car while his son-in-law and I talked. The older man could see you in the window." Lin gestured to the window overlooking Main Street.

A rush of cold air flooded the room causing Lin to be hopeful that the ghost might be ready to appear, but he didn't become visible.

"Were you fond of the people who used to live here? Nicholas and Catherine Whittaker. They lived here for quite a long time. You must have been very used to them being in the house."

Loud knocking behind them made Lin and Viv jump.

"Is that a yes or a no?" Viv whispered.

"Not sure." Lin continued to talk to the spirit. "I found out that Catherine Whittaker was a direct descendant of the Bean family. And the man I was speaking with out front earlier, his wife Gemma is a distant relative of the Beans. Long ago, the Beans owned the land this house is built on. And in fact, a man named George Bean purchased the land in the 1800s and was the one who had this house built."

The house shook and quaked as if an earthquake were taking place on the island, and Viv clutched her cousin's arm.

"What's going on? Should we run?"

Lin shook her head. "We'll be okay. Something I said touched a nerve."

Slowly, the vibration in the house subsided.

"The older man in the car could see you, but I can't," Lin told the ghost. "I know you want help from us. Maybe it would be helpful, if you could become visible to us? That way, we could look at old photographs and try to find out your name. Unless you could write your name on the paper on the desk?"

Lin could see a little shimmer of atoms by the desk, and she held her breath, ready to see the ghost take shape, but the only things that appeared were the paper and the pen, hanging suspended in the air. As she and Viv stepped closer, the piece of paper fluttered down to the desktop. They both watched as the pen jiggled a little, but then the point aimed toward the paper and gently floated down.

Lin held her breath as the pen shakily moved,

just a bit, on the paper. A small vertical line was drawn and the pen twitched and jerked as an attempt was made to place another mark beside the line.

When a car door slammed outside, Viv walked to the window and peered into the darkness where a Jeep was parked under the streetlight. "Michael and Eileen Salem are here."

A rumbling sound filled the air and the pen was forcefully thrown across the room and disappeared. The ghost wailed for several moments before quieting.

"Does he not like the Salems?" Viv asked.

"I think he's frustrated to be interrupted just when he was able to start controlling the pen."

They heard the front door open and the man called hello. "Lin? Viv? Are you upstairs?"

"We are," Lin responded.

When Michael came up the stairs and entered the room, he looked around. "Hey, there. What are you doing?"

"Just trying to make things better with the ghost," Lin gave the man a small smile.

"Any luck?"

"Some. We're heading out now."

Furious knocking began and it sounded as if multiple people were pounding on the walls.

Michael looked disgusted. "I wish this would stop." He had to raise his voice to be heard over the din. "Eileen is nearly at the end of her rope. She doesn't even want to come up here. She's staying on the first floor."

"Why don't we go downstairs," Viv suggested.

As they turned to leave the room, Lin glanced back at the desk and noticed the paper was still there. She quickly stepped closer and under the first vertical line written on the paper was a squiggly curved line that almost looked like an elaborate S.

Her heart dropped.

Too bad we got interrupted. The ghost was making progress with the writing.

She walked to the doorway and took another look back at the desk by the window.

The paper was gone.

Downstairs in the foyer, Michael was telling Viv that he'd stopped by to see how the restoration was progressing.

"How's Eileen?" Lin questioned. "You said she's down here?"

"Eileen needs a break from the house and its

ghost." Michael's facial muscles looked tense. "She went outside."

Lin felt her phone vibrating in her back pocket and took it out to see who was calling. Taking a quick read of the text message, the hand holding the phone abruptly dropped to her side.

"We need to go."

The tone of Lin's voice made Viv stand straight and examine her cousin's face trying to read what was wrong.

"We'll see you later." Lin turned on her heel and headed out with Viv right behind her.

Outside, hurrying down the walkway, Viv asked, "What's wrong?"

"April. There's been another incident."

The cousins practically jogged down the sidewalks to April's street and as they hurried along, Viv asked for details.

"That's all she said. *Please come. There's been another incident.*"

"Good grief." Viv puffed as they trotted up the sidewalks. "What could it be this time?"

April was on the front porch when Lin and Viv arrived at the house.

"Thank you for coming so fast." April's face was

ashen and her fingers shook as she pushed her hair back from her face.

"Is it another note?" Viv asked as she stepped up onto the porch.

"Come inside." April led them into the house and unlocked the door to her first floor apartment.

The place was cozy and nicely furnished with a modern area rug, a plush sofa and chairs, a non-working fireplace, some of April's handmade baskets, pretty lamps, bookshelves, and some oil paintings of ships on the walls.

The young woman led them into her bedroom.

"When I got home, I came in here to change and saw this." She pointed to one of the windows. The screen was partially knocked out and the window glass was smashed. "Someone tried to break in. Maybe he heard something and ran away. This was on the floor." She handed a small piece of paper to Lin so she and Viv could read it.

Lin read aloud the handwritten note, *"I told you not to date these worthless men. Maybe you need to be taught a lesson."* Something about the note, besides the obvious, picked at Lin.

Viv groaned. "Have you called the police?"

"No." April's voice was small.

"Call them. It was an attempted break-in. It's an

escalation to the notes. The police will come and take a look around."

"Okay." April made the call and when she hung up, she said, "A patrol car will be here in a few minutes."

"Good." Lin looked out the window. "I'd go outside to have a look around, but if there are footprints out there, I don't want to mess them up." She turned around. "You didn't see anyone?"

"No, I think they were trying to break in when I wasn't here. I just got home and saw this." April sank onto the bed. "I wish it would just stop."

"We talked to your friend Peter Norton out at his shop," Lin explained. "He didn't recall anyone from the past who might be doing this."

"Also," Viv added, "we don't think it's Peter who's responsible for the notes."

"Peter?" April's hand flew to her the side of her face. "I never suspected him. Gosh, you thought the Mailman might be Peter?"

"Anything's possible," Lin said simply. "I'm suspicious of everyone. Friends, neighbors, associates, customers ... family."

April shot to her feet. "Not my dad. No way. Wipe that thought from your mind right now."

"Weirder things have happened," Viv said softly.

"I know it seems harsh, but if we ignore people because they're close to you, then we might be allowing the perp to slip through our fingers."

"It's not my dad," April said firmly. "I was with him several times when the notes showed up. He couldn't have placed them in the mailbox when I was with him."

"Okay," Lin nodded and took out her phone. "I'm going to text my husband. He can come over and fix the window, or at least, board it up."

April softened. "Thank you."

When the doorbell rang, they went to meet the police officers. April explained what she'd found when she returned home and took them into the bedroom to show them the damage. "This note was on the floor by the window."

"We'd like to keep this," one officer said after reading it.

Lin stepped forward. "I'd like to photograph the note before you take it."

April looked surprised by Lin's comment, but she said nothing.

The officers asked questions and made notes, and then went outside to check the premises just as Jeff pulled up in his truck.

The three women went out to meet him and April explained the broken window and the note.

Anger flushed Jeff's face. "More needs to be done. We can't allow this to escalate to the point where someone gets hurt." He deliberately didn't say April was the someone who was going to get hurt.

"You're right," Lin said. "You're absolutely right."

16

Cisco Beach was on the southern side of the island near the end of Hummock Pond Road. Jason Price, twenty-six, lived in a ranch house on a quiet lane off Hummock Pond. The man was handsome, tall, with jet black hair and dark eyes. He opened the door quickly after Lin pressed the bell.

The cousins introduced themselves and Jason led them through a well-tended and nicely deco-rated living room, dining room, and kitchen and out to the covered patio.

"My wife will be back soon with the kids so it will probably be quieter if we sit outside." Jason smiled.

"How many kids do you have?" Viv asked.

"Two. They're twins. A boy and a girl. They're

three years old. My wife and I got married at twenty-two and had the kids the next year. It's been a whirl-wind, but I wouldn't have it any other way." Jason looked happy as he spoke about his family. "Can I get you something to drink?"

"We're good, thanks," Lin said.

"So you said when you called that you're talking to former classmates of Julie Blake. What's going on? Is she in some sort of trouble?"

"Back in high school, did you know someone was delivering notes to the Blakes' mailbox? Most were addressed to Julie, but others were sent to her sisters."

"What kind of notes?"

"The notes complimented the sisters' looks, mentioned their activities, commented on what they'd been wearing. It was clearly someone who was familiar with them." Viv gave the explanation with an even tone of voice. If Jason was the author of the notes, she didn't want to spook him.

"And what? The person put the notes in their mailbox?"

"Yes. On a fairly regular basis," Lin told him. "The family felt it was harassing behavior."

"Were threats made to the family?" Jason asked.

"Not until recently."

"Recently? You mean this has been going on for … for years?" Jason's eyes had widened.

Lin nodded.

"What about the police? This is a small island. The person hasn't been caught?"

Ignoring the question, Lin asked, "You didn't know about this? When you were in high school?"

"I didn't know. I was a quiet, shy kid back then. I didn't have a lot of friends. The kids I hung out with weren't socially outgoing so it doesn't surprise me that we hadn't heard about it."

"You dated Julie back then?" Viv leaned back against the chair cushion.

"Yeah, we went out a couple of times. I thought Julie was a goddess. I was practically tongue-tied around her." Jason smiled and shook his head. "The way I behaved around her could have been the inspiration for one of those high school movies about an awkward nerd-kid who gets to date the prom queen. *I* would have dumped me."

"If you were so awkward, how did you get Julie to go out on a date with you?" Lin sincerely wondered how that played out.

"Back then, I was a good-looking guy. I was smart. Julie was in some of my classes. One day, she dropped her books and I picked them up for her, then I blurted out how I wondered if she'd like to go a movie. When she said yes, I nearly fainted." Jason chuckled. "We had two or three dates and that was it. It was like I was mute when I was around her. It was embarrassing."

"I think we've all felt like that at one time or another." Lin gave him a warm smile.

"When you think back on your senior year, can you recall anyone who seemed too interested in Julie?"

"Me?" Jason shook his head.

"Anyone else?" Viv asked. "Another student, a staff member, a coach?"

Jason looked out over the yard while he gave the question some thought. "I wasn't really in the mix of things in high school. I didn't see Julie much outside of our classes. I can't think of anything that seemed inappropriate or unusual about how the teachers interacted with her. You think the note-writer was someone at the high school?"

"We can't be sure, but the notes started during Julie's senior year. We thought we'd ask around, see if anyone noticed anything."

"And the notes are still arriving after all this time?"

"They're addressed to April now."

Jason rolled his eyes. "This is ridiculous. It's … creepy." He sat up. "Julie and her sisters worked at the family restaurant. Do you think it could be a customer? It's always been a busy place. The girls might have caught someone's eye."

"It's sure possible," Viv said.

After another thirty minutes of conversation, Jason's wife, Randi, and the kids came home. The boy and girl were dark-haired and adorable and chattered away at Viv and Lin. They were both smart and well-mannered. Randi was a nurse at the hospital and talked about how busy the place was in the summer when the tourists descended on the island, and how she picked up more hours.

"When the slower seasons get here, I'm ready for a vacation," she laughed.

Jason walked the cousins out to Lin's truck.

"I'm sorry I couldn't be of any help. I hope you figure something out so the guy gets caught. If there's any way I can help out, just give me a call. This has got to stop."

In the truck heading back toward town, Viv said, "Jason seems really nice. I was being careful not to get sucked in by his niceness in case he was trying to throw us off. I sincerely believe he had nothing to do with the notes."

"I agree. He was honest, upfront. I don't think he's the perp. It was a longshot, but I hoped we'd get lucky and we'd find one person who noticed something that seemed off about someone back then. It's like a needle in a haystack."

Viv rubbed her temples. "I bet the perp is someone who everyone thinks is so great and upstanding. He's got to be really smart and extremely careful. All these years, and he's never been caught."

Lin was quiet for a few minutes. "I wish we hadn't been interrupted by Michael Salem the other evening. I think our ghost was getting the hang of moving the pen. I think he would have been able to write a word or two."

"Why don't we stop by the house on the way home?" Viv suggested as she checked the time. "Will the work crew be done for the day?"

"They will be. Jeff told me they'd be going to another house they're restoring later in the afternoon. They're going full out. They need to hire more workers, but nothing has worked out so far."

Ten minutes later, they were parked in front of the Main Street house where they went in and climbed the stairs to the second floor.

All was quiet until Lin spoke. "We're here. It's Lin and Viv. Are you there?"

Footsteps thunked over the floor without a body to be seen. To the window, to the desk, to the doorway, the ghost made a circle around the room, over and over again.

"When we were here before, it seemed you might write something more on the paper. Would you like to try again?" Lin moved her eyes around the room hoping to see some shimmering particles.

The footsteps stopped and the room was so quiet, Lin could hear her own breathing.

The pen and paper appeared on the desk, and in a moment, the pen was lifted up and touched the paper. It moved slowly, as if whoever held it was having a tremendously hard time handling the pen.

The paper still had the ink mark that the ghost made the last time the cousins were there.

The jiggling pen made a second vertical mark on the paper and then connected the the two with a horizontal line.

"An H?" Lin asked.

The tip of the pen hit the paper several times, hard.

"Not an H?" Viv asked.

The pen pounded against the paper.

"Okay, wait. Is it an A?" Lin asked hopefully.

The pen was gently put down.

Viv examined the marks. "So this is an A. What about this squiggly line under it? Is this an S? Are these your initials?"

The pen rose in the air and then pounded against the S.

"Okay, so they're not your initials?" Lin asked.

The pen bounced hotly between the two letters and Lin and Viv looked at one another helplessly.

"Can you add more letters to the message?"

The pen hung suspended in mid-air. An unseen hand guided the pen down and tried to write another letter on the paper, but the pen wobbled and wiggled and nothing intelligible could be managed.

Footsteps pounded the floor as the ghost paced back and forth, clearly frustrated by his inability to write more letters.

"It's okay. It's a hard task. A little bit at a time. We won't give up," Lin spoke. "You'll be able to do it soon."

Viv leaned close and whispered, "Ask him if he can show himself."

"Would you like to appear to us?"

Near the window, some particles caught the light

and began to shimmer. They started to swirl and grow brighter, but in a moment, they sparked like tiny ashes blown away by a breeze.

"It's okay. I know its hard. It takes a lot of energy to materialize." Lin didn't know that for sure, but over the years, it seemed to be so. "Maybe next time we come."

The pen on the desk lifted one more time, and it hit the letter "S" again and again.

"We'll figure it out. We won't give up," Lin used a calming voice. It was clear the ghost was trying hard to get a message across. It would take a little longer to decipher what it was.

A shiver ran over Lin's skin.

Why does it seem like we're running out of time?

17

It was dark outside when Lin walked into Viv's bookstore and headed to the back where the café was located. Since Jeff and John were working late again, the cousins decided they'd take a stroll through town and maybe, stop in to hear a band playing at one of the pubs. Lin spotted Viv and Anton sitting at one of the tables so she went over to join them.

"We were just talking about you." Anton set down his coffee mug. "Viv was telling me that the new ghost is attempting communication by writing to you. Fascinating. I would love to see this."

"Come with us next time we go to the house," Lin suggested.

"It can be scary sometimes," Viv told him. "You

just have to be ready for loud noises and some occasional wailing."

"I think I could handle that." Anton adjusted his eyeglasses. "I've never really been close to a ghost."

"Well, this can be your chance. I don't think he'd be bothered by your presence."

"When can I join you?" Anton looked at his appointment book. "It can't be tomorrow evening. Libby and I have been invited to a garden party."

"Have you?" Viv looked surprised. "So have we. At the Linton-Campbells?"

"Yes, you're going?" Anton's face lit up. "Excellent." He turned to Lin. "You, too?"

"Jeff and I, Viv and John, and Leonard and Heather. Leonard and I have been hired to do some landscaping for them." Lin leaned closer to the man. "When we were there to talk to Thomas about the project, he took us down to the inner harbor. His property borders the water. I went out on a small wooden dock and I had such a feeling of anxiety and dread that I had to get out of there ... fast. It was that disturbing."

"What was the cause? Do you know?"

Lin shook her head. "Maybe tomorrow, we can go down there. I'd like to take Libby to the dock and see if she senses something similar."

"You'll probably be able to walk down to the dock," Anton guessed. "There will be over a hundred people there. I don't think anyone will be keeping tabs on the guests."

"I hope not. Something isn't right at that dock." Lin's face had clouded with the memory of the experience. "I hope Thomas hasn't done something bad down there. He seems like such a nice man."

"Maybe between you and Viv and Libby, you'll be able to figure out why the dock is so upsetting," Anton said. "Oh, look. Speak of the devil. Here comes Libby now."

The woman hurried to the table, sat, and reached for Anton's coffee mug.

"Help yourself." Anton raised an eyebrow. "Oh, I see you already have."

"Don't be fussy," she told him. "The coffee's cold anyway." She looked to Viv and Lin. "I was hoping Viv was still here. Lin being here, too, is a bonus. I met with a woman who was working as a home health aide for Nicholas and Catherine Whittaker before they passed. She's willing to speak with you about them. Perhaps you can find out something about the ghost."

"That's great," Lin smiled. "Do you have her

contact information? We can reach out and set up a meeting."

"No need. I've already done that."

"Done what?" Viv was confused.

"I've set up a meeting for you two to meet the woman."

"Okay, when is it?"

"In thirty minutes."

Lin tilted her head to the side. "Right now?"

"She has the evening free. She runs a home health care company and she's extremely busy all the time. I had to take advantage of her having a few free hours," Libby defended herself.

Viv said, "Lin and I had plans for the evening, but I guess this is more important."

"It is." Libby took another swallow of the cold coffee.

"I can get you your own beverage, you know," Viv told the woman.

"Could you? I really need some caffeine. But hurry. You don't want to keep Joyce waiting."

Viv suppressed a sigh and got up to get the coffee.

"That's the home health care person's name? Joyce?" Lin asked.

"Joyce Simone. I've only met her once, but she

seems very nice. She might be helpful. It's worth meeting her to see what she can tell you about the Whittakers."

Viv brought a steaming mug to the table and Libby sipped. "Delicious. I was too busy today. It wore me out. I was dragging when I got here. Anyway, it's nice to see you both. You'd better get going. Let me know how it goes."

Once outside, Viv chuckled. "Libby's a character. She can be very single-minded. It didn't matter if we had other plans. She practically commanded us to go meet this woman. Oh, wait, did she give you the address?"

"She did. She *is* a character, but she's always helpful. I don't know what I would have done without her when I came back to the island. Libby really helped me accept my skills."

"She's been invaluable to you. You know I love the old bat," Viv grinned.

The cousins walked through the neighborhoods at the edge of town, and Joyce Simone's house was only about a quarter of a mile from Viv's house. They approached a small pretty one-story home that had a stone walkway to the front door and flower gardens covering the front yard. Two lampposts lit the way along the curved walk.

It only took less than a minute for Joyce to open the door after they rang the doorbell. Joyce looked to be in her mid-forties. She was petite, had shoulder-length wavy dark brown hair, skin the color of dark caramel, and almond-shaped brown eyes.

"It's Lin and Viv, right? I'm Joyce. Libby told me about you. Please come in."

Joyce led them into a cream-colored living room with soft plush beige sofas that were set in front of a fireplace. Colorful artwork hung on the walls, and an area rug with brown and sage patterns in it was soft underfoot.

"Please, sit."

There was a pot of tea on the table and Joyce poured three cups. "There're sugar cubes in the bowl and cream in the silver pot. Libby told me your husband is doing restoration work on the house that used to belong to the Whittakers."

"He is. Jeff has a lot going on right now. He and his partner have bitten off more than they can comfortably chew, but it will all work out," Lin said. "You worked with the Whittakers for a while?"

"I did," Joyce smiled. "They were lovely people. I worked with them for five years. Nicholas passed about eight months before Catherine. She had a hard time with her husband's death. She was never herself after that. She went right downhill when she lost him."

"That's very sad," Viv said.

"They were in their nineties when they died. They had good, long lives."

"We understand there were no children," Lin said. "And no living relatives at all."

"That's right. Catherine told me they tried to have a family, but it was not to be. They were both quite sorrowful about that, but they accepted it and built good lives together. They were extremely generous to the island community and to the city of Boston, where they lived for decades. They gave millions and millions of dollars to worthy causes during their lifetimes and for the most part, donated their estate to charity. They did remember some close friends and some of us who took care of them in their will. I have to say I was shocked to be named in their will."

"They sound like very caring and generous people," Lin nodded.

"I grew close to them over the years."

"Mrs. Whittaker was a descendant of the Bean family?" Viv brought up the subject.

"She was." Joyce smiled and shook her head.

"She wasn't crazy about being a Bean. She told me many of the Beans were not good people."

"How did she mean?" Lin looked closely at Joyce.

"She told me that some of them were cheats and scoundrels. Her words. She said all they cared about was money, position, and power. She was grateful for the good fortune that came to her for being a Bean, but she believed you could be successful without taking advantage of others."

"She was right," Viv agreed.

"She certainly was," Joyce said.

"What did Mr. Whittaker do for work?" Lin asked.

"Nicholas owned an investment firm. He founded it himself. The couple lived in Boston until he sold the company. That's when they moved to Nantucket full time. They owned the house on Main Street for decades. They'd spend most of their time here in the summer."

"Did they know some history of the house? It had been in the Bean family since the 1830s," Lin said.

"Catherine knew quite a bit about the house. She'd drop interesting tidbits in our conversations."

"Some people say there's a ghost who lives there," Viv broached the subject.

"Well, people say all kinds of things." Joyce waved her hand around.

"Nantucket is known to have quite a few ghostly sightings." Lin tried to word her comment in the right way. "Did Catherine ever mention a ghost?"

Joyce smiled. "She did, in fact. She believed spirits walked the earth. She told me there was a shy, sweet ghost who lived with them."

"Did she have any guesses as to why there was a ghost who wouldn't leave?" Lin questioned.

"She called the ghost the *Poor One*. I think she had some idea who might be haunting the place, but she kept it to herself."

"Why do you think she knew something about the ghost?"

"One day, I heard her mumbling and I asked if she was talking to me. She told me she was only speaking with the Poor One ... he never got to live his life."

"Do you know if he had taken ill during his life?"

"I asked questions, but Catherine kept the information to herself. Maybe it was just the delusions of an old woman." Joyce shrugged.

"Did you ever sense the ghost?" Viv asked.

"A few times, I felt I'd walked into a cold pocket

of air. It made me shiver. But, I know it was my imagination."

"Did Catherine have any close friends on-island?"

"Yes, she did. Most of them have passed away. One person she was close to is still living in Tom Nevers. She's in her nineties, but doing well. Her name is Elizabeth Hanes. I don't know much of anything about the Whittakers' house. Libby said you were interested in its history. I don't know any more about the place, but maybe Mrs. Hanes could tell you more. I don't have her contact information, but she should be easy to find. Catherine and Elizabeth were like sisters. I bet she could answer some of your questions."

I just hope she knows something about the Poor One, Lin thought.

18

Following a long line of cars and trucks, Jeff turned off the truck's engine and he, Lin, Viv, and John stepped out and waited for Heather and Leonard to emerge from their stopped car in the driveway of the Linton-Campbells mansion. Valet drivers took the keys and drove the vehicles away to a parking area.

"Wow, this is amazing." Viv stood staring at the huge estate. White twinkling lights were wound around tree trunks, boughs, and bushes making the place look magical. Torches lit the way along the stone walkways to the rear of the property, and the six friends followed along after the other party-goers.

"I'd love to broker the sale of this house." John was practically salivating from the idea of being the real estate agent who held the listing for the mansion.

"I don't think the Linton-Campbells have any intention of selling this property," Lin smiled.

"One can dream." John's head practically swiveled as he looked over the place.

"I was here once before," Heather told them. "Thomas and Gemma sure know how to throw a party."

"Do they need any renovations or restoration work done?" Jeff joked, imagining getting the contract to do work on the house.

Leonard said, "If we hear the couple wants some work done, we'll be sure to send them to you and Kurt."

At the rear of the house, there was a huge white tent in the middle of the yard with a dance floor at one end and drinks and hors d'oeuvres and desserts at the other side. Chandeliers hung from the ceiling illuminating the party in a soft golden glow, and a wooden deck stood off the end of the tent floor. Urns of flowers, arbors covered with flowers and ivy, ice sculptures, lanterns, and torches decorated the yard. Men and women carrying silver trays with drinks and appetizers strolled around amongst the guests to offer them beverages or bites to eat. A band played near the dance floor and the people's chatter and laughter filled the air.

The men wore suits, mostly without ties, and the women had on summery cocktail dresses and sandals. Lin wore a pale yellow dress with swirls of pastel colors on the fabric, Viv had on a mid-calf sleeveless violet dress that had ruching around the chest, and Heather wore a cream-colored fitted dress with red accents.

"This is going to be fun," John grinned.

"Where should we start?" Jeff asked.

"The food table." Leonard took Heather's hand and started across the lawn. "If I have to wear this monkey suit, then I need something to eat to comfort me."

The others chuckled and followed after them.

"Libby and Anton are over there by the drink tables," Lin pointed out and the group walked over to join them.

"Quite a turnout." Anton sipped from his drink. "You all look very nice."

"I love your dress," Heather told Libby who wore a royal blue dress with a fitted bodice and a flared skirt.

The group chatted for several minutes before

Thomas and Gemma Linton-Campbell came over to join the conversation.

Thomas introduced Lin and Leonard to his wife.

"Thomas was very impressed with both of you. I'm so glad you could make it to our party."

Viv, John, Jeff, and Heather were introduced to the couple.

The eight people formed smaller groups of two or three and began separate conversations.

"Your husband told us that you're a descendant of the Bean family," Lin said to Gemma.

In her sixties, the woman was slim, had blond hair held up in a twisted chignon, and dark brown eyes. Her nails were nicely manicured with pale polish and she wore an ankle-length rose-colored dress that fit and draped perfectly. Lin was pretty sure the dress must have cost what she herself made in a month.

Gemma gave Lin a soft smile. "The Bean family spread out far and wide. There are probably millions of us," she exaggerated. "The early Beans were unethical and power-hungry. The family isn't anything I like to associate myself with."

"There must be quite a few people on Nantucket with Bean ancestry."

Gemma nodded. "Probably every other person you bump into walking around town."

"Thomas told us that one of the Beans owned this property generations ago," Lin said.

"I wasn't pleased to hear that when we were buying the place. Thomas mentioned that your husband has the contract to restore the house that Nicholas and Catherine Whittaker owned. George Bean had that house built. He was the one who owned this parcel in the early 1830s."

A little shiver slipped over Lin's arms. "Did he?"

Gemma gave a nod. "He owned ships, shops in town, land. From stories passed down, it's clear that ole George was a cheat and a liar and the only things that mattered to him were money and more money. Thankfully, my Bean blood is pretty well diluted."

"What were the stories about him?" Lin questioned, eager to hear what the woman had to say about an ancestor.

Just then, Thomas interrupted them. "Excuse me, Lin, I'm going to steal my wife away for a little while. We need to mingle around and make sure we speak to all our guests. We'll circle back around to chat with all of you in a bit."

Lin gave the man a smile. "We'll look forward to catching up with you later."

As the Linton-Campbells walked away, Michael and Eileen Salem walked up.

"I didn't know you knew our hosts," Michael said to Lin after shaking hands with everyone in the group.

"Leonard and I have contracted with them to create some new gardens."

"New gardens?" Eileen scoffed. "How many gardens does someone need? It seems like overkill."

Lin didn't care for the comment, but kept her opinion to herself. "It's a large yard. There are plenty of spaces that can be converted into gardens. Thomas doesn't care for the idea of extensive lawns. He'd prefer to offer food and habitat to birds, butterflies, and other wildlife."

"Thomas is definitely a tree hugger," Eileen said with a slight frown. "He thinks he can save the world."

"Well," Lin said, "maybe a small part of it."

Eileen moved closer to Lin. "It seems like our resident ghost is getting worse. When we go into the house, the spirit carries on something terrible." The woman wrung her hands. "I don't know what we're going to do if you're unable to get the ghost to quiet down. We lived in harmony with the spirit in our other house. I thought we could do the same thing in our new home. I told Michael we'll have to sell if the ghost continues to haunt the place."

"These things take time," Lin explained as best she could. "Each spirit is different, and has different needs. It can take a while to figure out what a ghost wants."

"I hope it doesn't take too long. I can't stand hearing the noises and sounds the ghost makes. It makes my skin crawl. I'm afraid he's going to hurt us."

"I don't think that's his intention. I think he's so upset with what happened to him that he can't control his behavior. When things start to settle and he gets to know you, he'll get used to the way things are going to be."

"You're far more patient than I am," Eileen admitted. "I hope you're right. I didn't want to come to this party. I have to get up for the early ferry back to the mainland."

"Are you going to spend some time on Cape Cod?"

"Oh gosh, no. I have meetings tomorrow with clients."

Lin's was intrigued. "What do you do for work?"

"I'm an attorney. Personal injury. I have a firm in Boston with a team of twenty. I can usually do everything over the internet, but tomorrow some meetings require me to be present in the office."

"It sounds interesting," Lin told her.

"It can be."

"Is Michael an attorney as well?"

"He isn't, thankfully. He's a business professor at MIT. He's written books, does consulting."

Right then, Michael stepped over to chat with them. "Discussing business?"

"Not really." Eileen took a sip from the glass she was holding. "I was just complaining about having to take the early ferry in the morning."

"Fly instead," Michael suggested.

"That won't get me there any earlier."

"How long have you been at MIT?" Lin asked.

"About twelve years. Before that we were in California. It was a good opportunity here in the East, so we took it. We fell in love with Nantucket the first time we saw it and bought a house here. If we hadn't moved east, we would never have been able to live on this little piece of paradise."

"We have an apartment in Boston for when we have to be there," Eileen said. "I hope the restoration goes smoothly. I'm already getting tired of living in the rental house."

"You're lucky to have two homes to split your

time between. Where on-island was the house you owned before buying the Main Street house?"

Michael said, "In one of the edge of town neighborhoods."

Jeff walked over to join them. "I was wondering if I could borrow my wife. I'd like to dance with her."

"Of course," Michael nodded. "There are some people we need to meet up with. Have a good time. Nice to talk with you." He and Eileen went off across the lawn.

"Sorry to interrupt." Jeff took Lin's hand and kissed her palm.

"You're never interrupting." Lin put her arm around her husband's waist and they headed for the dance floor. "Something the Salems said made me feel like I should ask them a question, but whatever it was, it slipped right out of my mind before I could do it."

"You'll think of it."

"Yeah. But it's probably not important."

Or is it?

19

Lin and Jeff danced alongside their friends under the warm light of the chandeliers. It was a perfect summer evening with good friends, good food, enjoyable conversation, and beautiful surroundings under a moonlit sky. After finishing a slow dance together and walking off the dance floor, Libby and Anton approached.

"It's getting late." Libby glanced around. "If you want to go down to the dock, we'd better do it now."

A rush of anxiety ran through Lin's veins as her soaring spirits came crashing down. The fun evening was coming to an end.

"Okay. I'll get Viv and John."

One of Anton's eyebrows went up. "John? He won't want to be involved in this."

"I'll give him the option. Why don't you two wander over to the trail that leads down to the inner harbor." Lin had pointed out the trailhead to her friends when they first arrived. "It will be less conspicuous to the other guests if we walk over there in pairs."

While Lin and Jeff went to fetch the other two, Libby and Anton strolled over to the trail, and when it seemed like no one was watching, they walked several yards into the trees. In no time, Lin, Jeff, and Viv met them on the winding path. Leonard stayed behind with Heather since the woman had no idea that some of their friends could see ghosts.

"You were right about John," Lin told Anton.

"He's going to mingle with the guests," Viv said. "He's always looking to make new contacts."

"The young man is smart and ambitious," Libby nodded. "Lead the way, Lin."

Taking a deep breath, Lin moved slowly down the path with the others behind her. Lin had worn flat sandals in anticipation, and Libby had done the same. The moonlight lit up the trail fairly well and they used their phone flashlights to help with any dark spots or rough terrain.

"Here we are." Lin held back from getting close to the dock.

"Wow, this is gorgeous. What a view of the harbor." Viv drank in the sight of the moonglow falling on the water, lighting up a glistening path over the calm, quiet inner harbor.

Libby was more matter-of-fact. "Let's try to figure out what Lin felt the last time she was here." She addressed the young woman. "I'm picking up on your anxiety. Acknowledge your apprehension, but don't allow it to get the better of you. You'll be able to do this. We're with you." The older woman started down the dock and when she got to the end, she turned around and took hold of Lin's hands.

Libby looked at Jeff and Anton who stood back. "Do you gentleman want to join us? The more energy we have to call on, the better this will go."

"Jeff is beginning to notice the shimmering when a ghost is ready to appear," Lin said. "He might be able to help add to our power."

"And Anton understands what we do and always gives positive energy," Viv agreed. "Both men can help us. Do you want to join the circle?" she asked them.

Jeff and Anton came forward. Jeff held hands with Lin and Viv, and Anton took hold of Viv's and Libby's hands. Because the dock was small in width, the small group had to form sort of an oblong configuration instead of a circle, but Libby told them it would work just as well.

They closed their eyes and focused on their breathing as the night sounds surrounded them ... the gentle lapping of the water, the slight movement of the dock, the hoot of an owl, the rhythmic buzz of crickets or bugs calling to one another.

Lin could feel herself drifting away, and then a terrible sense of dread and danger pummeled her. She felt herself fall into the cold, dark water ... she wanted to stroke with her arms so she could push to the surface, but they wouldn't move. Down, down, she went, everything turning to black.

She gasped and pulled her hands away from Jeff and Libby. Before she could fall from the dock, Jeff embraced his wife.

"Lin, Lin. It's okay. You're here with me."

At the same time, Libby's eyes popped open as she took a quick step back and almost lost her balance and slipped from the dock, but Anton and Viv grabbed her before she fell.

"Hello," a voice called from the shore. Thomas Linton-Campbell stood there with a flashlight in his hand sweeping the light over the people on the dock.

Viv smiled at the man and shaded her eyes from the light. "Hi there. When Lin was here before, she fell in love with this spot. She wanted to take us down to see it." The young woman and Anton walked quickly down the dock to the sandy edge of the shoreline. "It's simply a perfect place."

"It's been a very enjoyable evening," Anton told Thomas. "Thank you for your hospitality."

The others came slowly off the dock. Feeling woozy, Lin held tight to Jeff's arm.

"I hope you don't mind that we came down here. I should have asked you if it was all right."

"Not at all," Thomas said. "I noticed you and your husband taking the path. I thought I'd check to be sure you were okay."

"Is the party moving down here?" Michael and Eileen Salem came onto the shore from the trail.

"Oh, hello." Thomas turned around to see who was approaching. "Michael. Eileen. It seems everyone wants to see the harbor this evening."

Anton said, "It's a beautiful sight with the moonlight on the ocean."

Eileen stepped closer to Thomas. "When your wife hosted the garden club a while back, she brought us down here to see the water. Gemma told us you like to come down in the evenings with mugs of tea and sit on the dock. I wanted to show the spot to Michael."

They all chatted together for a little while before Lin said, "Well, we need to head out. Some of us have very early mornings tomorrow. Thank you so much for inviting us."

They made their way along the trail and returned to the manicured grounds of the Linton-Campbell estate.

"I need a drink of water before we go." Lin pressed her fingers against her temple.

"Is a headache coming on?" Libby asked.

"It is." Lin's voice was soft.

"I feel the same thing." Libby slipped her arm through Anton's so she could lean on him a bit. "What did you feel on the dock?"

Lin took in a deep breath. She didn't like reliving the sensations. "I felt like I fell into the water. I was sinking. I tried to swim, but my limbs wouldn't move."

Libby nodded. "And then, everything went black."

Lin stopped walking and made eye contact with the older woman. "Yes," she whispered.

"I had the exact same vision," Libby said as they continued toward the tent and the beverage tables. "Did anyone else sense something?"

Viv said, "I felt nervous and afraid. Not my usual

apprehension about having ghosts around. I sensed danger. I had the urge to get out of there."

"I felt something similar," Jeff agreed. "Almost fearful."

"I could feel what seemed like a tiny electric current buzzing through my hands, but no sense of dread or fear," Anton explained.

"What do you make of it?" Libby asked Lin.

Lin cleared her throat. "I think ... I think someone died back there."

Libby's eyes clouded and then she sighed. "I think that the person we sensed was already dead before they hit the water."

All eyes turned to the woman.

Anton adjusted his eyeglasses. "Murder, then?"

With an expression of sadness moving over her face, Libby nodded. "Definitely."

After collecting the truck from the valet, Lin, Jeff, Viv, and John climbed inside and Jeff turned the steering wheel and followed the long driveway out to the road. As soon as they left the estate, Lin felt her phone buzzing in her clutch.

"It's April." Lin's heart dropped. "There's another

note. She found it a few minutes ago. It was taped to her apartment door."

"Her apartment door?" Viv was alarmed. "That means the person got into the house. The front door is locked. You need a key to get in."

"Are there buzzers near the front door?" John asked. "Is there an intercom? Can someone buzz in a visitor or does someone have to go to the door and open it for them?"

"I don't remember," Lin said. "April is asking if we can come by."

"Absolutely." Jeff turned onto a different road than the one he was planning on taking and in fifteen minutes, they arrived in front of April's building.

Lin texted April to tell her they'd arrived, and by the time the four of them went to the front door of the big house, the young woman was opening it.

"There isn't an intercom or buzzers to open the door out here," John noted.

"I'm so sorry to bother you again so late." April's face was lined with worry. "There was another note. It was taped to my door."

They went with April into her apartment and sat down.

"How did he get in here to put the note on my door?" April was close to shaking.

"He could have come in with another resident of the building," Jeff suggested.

"If he did, then someone saw him." Lin sat up in excitement. "What time is it? Do you know your neighbors well enough to talk to them right now? Ask if any of them let a man into the house."

April checked the time. "It's kind of late. I could listen at their doors for the sounds of the television or voices. I can try."

Jeff stood. "I'll go with you."

The others waited in the living room, but Lin couldn't sit still so she paced back and forth until April and Jeff came back.

"Three people were at home. One was out," April reported. "No one we spoke to let anyone into the house. I can check with the other woman in the morning. It most likely means he picked the lock."

"I checked the lock before we came in," Jeff said. "It doesn't look like it was tampered with. Maybe the guy knows his way around locks."

"That doesn't make me feel great." April put her head in her hands.

"You haven't shown us the note," Lin told her.

"Oh. I'm so wound up. I left it on my dresser." April was back with the note in seconds and she handed it to Lin who read it aloud for everyone to hear.

"Things are coming to a head. I'll be back. Very soon."

Lin's breath caught in her throat as her stomach clenched.

20

It was early evening when Lin and Viv made their way to the church while discussing the previous night's event at April's apartment.

"How did the Mailman get inside the building? He must have picked the lock." Viv looked disgusted.

"I'd have to agree with that." Lin pulled her long hair up into a loose bun. "Jeff is installing a deadbolt on April's apartment door later today. The perp might be able to pick a lock on the front door, but with a deadbolt, it won't matter if he picks the apartment lock. The bolt will keep him from getting inside."

"Thank heavens. If I were April, I would have run, not walked, back to my parent's house."

"I think I would have done the same," Lin admitted.

"But I understand April not wanting to allow the Mailman to ruin her life. She doesn't want to huddle inside in fear. I took a photo of the note last night. There's something unusual about the way the Mailman writes his letters. It has a distinctive look to it."

"I looked at that note several times, and didn't notice anything unusual."

"I'll show you what I mean later. Here we are. Bill Barre told me he'd meet us in the church." Lin and her cousin went up the granite steps and opened the big wooden door.

Inside, the walls were painted white, there were high ceilings painted to show angels coming down from the sky, chandeliers lit the space, and a simple altar and a wooden pulpit stood to the side.

"Hello, there."

The cousins turned to the voice to see Bill Barre coming over to greet them. The man was in his late forties, was tall, was beginning to bald, and had a slight middle-age paunch. He smiled and shook hands with the young women.

"Why don't we go up to the choir loft. That way, we won't disturb anyone who comes in to pray." Bill gestured toward the staircase.

They took chairs near the organ.

"The organ is beautiful," Viv said.

"I've been playing here for over a decade. I love this organ." Bill ran his hand over a few of the keys, and then sat across from the cousins. "So you want to talk about the Blake family?"

"We would. Specifically, about the sisters." Lin smiled to try to put the man at ease.

"You probably know that the Blake sisters have been receiving anonymous notes from someone for about eight years," Viv explained.

"I heard Julie had a secret admirer."

"It's far more than a secret admirer," Lin pointed out. "It borders on criminal. The person is harassing the sisters, putting them in fear. The police have been contacted."

"I didn't know how serious it was." Bill scrunched up his forehead.

"It is, unfortunately. The notes have been arriving fairly regularly for eight years with some breaks from time to time. First, Julie was the initial target, then when she went off to school, Molly and Mallory received the bulk of the letters. Now, April is the unlucky recipient."

"Are the sisters being threatened?" Bill asked with interest.

"The whole thing can be considered threatening," Viv said. "It could escalate at any time."

"But it's been going on for eight years." Bill lifted his hands. "Nothing has escalated yet."

Viv's cheeks reddened in annoyance. "So do you think receiving strange notes for a decade isn't an odd, worrisome occurrence?"

Bill gave a shrug. "I'd say it was most likely harmless. Some oddball is trying to connect with four pretty girls. He admires them from a distance. It's like having fans, being a celebrity."

"Except the sisters are not celebrities and have not done anything to encourage a *fan*." Viv's voice had an edge to it. "It's concerning behavior that often leads to escalation. The thrill of leaving notes wears off and the culprit tries to recapture the rush he used to feel by doing something new."

Lin re-directed the conversation. "When did you first meet Julie?"

"The family attends church here on a regular basis. I came to the island about twelve years ago and joined the church about ten years ago as the organist. I knew the Blakes from attending services here."

"Did Julie sing in the choir?"

"She didn't. I heard her sing at a school concert.

The girl is talented. I begged her to join our choir, but she wasn't interested." Bill looked wistful. "She has the voice of an angel."

Lin felt something picking at her skin.

"What about the other sisters? Did they sing in the choir?"

"No. I never heard them sing, but I would expect their voices to be similar to their older sister. I invited them to join, but they didn't want to do it either. I admit I was very disappointed."

"Did you try to convince them?"

"I sure did. I spoke with them every Sunday. I didn't want to give up, but finally, I had to. There was no changing their minds."

Lin asked," Where did you live before coming to the island?"

"I lived outside of Boston. I was a high school teacher." Bill's face took on a sheepish expression. "I won the lottery."

Lin sat up. "Did you?"

"It wasn't a huge amount, but I was able to move here, buy a house. After a while, I missed teaching so I took a position at the island high school. I joined the church and accepted the opportunity to be the organist."

"Do you have a family?" Viv asked.

"I've never met the right woman. There's still time for me. I haven't given up hope." Bill nodded.

"Things can change in a heartbeat," Viv told him. "The right woman could come around the corner at any moment."

"I believe that's true," Bill smiled.

"Where do you live?" Lin questioned.

"Well, I used to live in the Blakes neighborhood at the edge of town, but five years ago, I moved into town. My house is only a few blocks from here and I like the convenience of being closer to the restaurants, coffee shops, market. My hip gives me trouble at times so I wanted to be able to easily stroll to everything I need."

"Is there anyone you can think of who might be sending the notes to the Blake sisters?" Lin closely watched the man's face for any hints of a reaction.

"Me?" Bill blinked. "I have no idea."

"Have you ever noticed someone who maybe stares at the sisters? Maybe tries to get close to them? Seems to have an unusual interest in them?"

"No," Bill seemed flustered as he began to stumble over his words. "I've never noticed anything like that ... I don't know ... nothing ... nothing seems off to me."

Outside after the interview, the cousins walked toward Main Street.

"I don't trust him." Viv rubbed at the back of her neck.

"Why not?" Lin felt the same way, but she wanted to hear Viv's thoughts.

"He seems evasive. At times, he acted a little nervous. He lived in the Blakes neighborhood for the first five years when the family was receiving the notes. I'd put him on the suspect list."

"And he taught at the high school when Julie was there," Lin added. "He might have seen her around school frequently, and she attended services at the church and he tried to get her to join the choir. It could be very innocent, but maybe not."

Viv gave her cousin a look. "And why did he *really* move into town? Was he worried the Blakes would find out he was the Mailman since he was right in their neighborhood?"

Lin pondered the comment. "It's possible."

"And his talk about having a hip problem might be a lie," Viv continued. "I didn't notice any limping when he walked around or climbed the stairs to the choir loft."

"You're right."

They arrived outside of Viv's house and got into her car that was parked in the driveway. They'd decided to take Viv's vehicle because it was less conspicuous than a truck and would be easier to park on the street.

"I'm not looking forward to this." Viv backed the car out of the driveway.

"Neither am I, but we have to do it. Jeff and John will take tomorrow night and the Blakes will take the night after that. With any luck, the Mailman will visit April's apartment house on one of the nights and one of us will get a look at him."

"Do you think he knows where we live?" Viv's voice revealed a tone of worry. "He must have seen us at April's place the first night she called us to come over. I bet he's been following us around to see if we're on to him. I bet he knows your truck and my car. If he sees my car, he'll walk away."

"In that case, we might have to set up a place to hide right outside the house," Lin suggested. "In the bushes or somewhere."

Viv rolled her eyes. "At least it's not the middle of winter."

Lin chuckled. "One thing in our favor."

Viv found a spot on the street close to April's apartment house. She parked facing down the slight hill so they would have a good view of the street and the front of the house.

"This is a good vantage point," Lin said. "We were lucky to get this spot."

Viv reached into the backseat for pillows and two blankets and Lin reached into the duffle bag that contained some snacks and a pair of binoculars. She pulled the binoculars out and set them on the console between the two front seats.

"Do you have a coin? We can flip it to see who stays awake for the first two hours."

Viv took a quarter from a small container on the dashboard. "You can call it." She tossed it and held it against the top of her hand.

"Tails."

"It's heads," Viv said. "I'm feeling hyped up and wired. I'll stay awake first."

Lin tucked the pillow against the passenger side door and pulled one of the blankets over herself.

"If you need me, just give me a little poke." Lin rested her head on the pillow.

"If I need you, I'll do more than that." Viv picked up the binoculars and began her watch.

21

Early the next morning, Lin and Viv returned to Viv's house where they had a quick breakfast. Nothing had happened during the night outside of April's place except for Viv's snoring, Lin having a nightmare, the car getting too stuffy to be comfortable, and both of them getting stiff necks or a crick in their backs.

Lin massaged her lower back. "I don't know how I'm going to get any work done today. My back is killing me."

"Call out sick?"

"Ha. Leonard would love it if I did that." Lin sipped her coffee.

"Maybe once you move around, your back will loosen up and feel better."

"I hope so." Lin dug into the pancakes. "But I think these blueberry pancakes might fix the back pain."

Cradling a coffee mug, Viv sat down at the kitchen table across from her cousin. "Do you think the Mailman saw us in the car last night? Is that why he didn't show up?"

"I guess he could have. It also might be that he's biding his time since he delivered the last note just the other night." Lin used her fork to dip a piece of pancake into a little puddle of maple syrup on her plate. "I need to go see the ghost soon. I haven't been to the Main Street house for a couple of days. I don't want him to think we deserted him."

"I'll go along. How about tomorrow evening? We have the meeting later today with Elizabeth Hanes."

"Okay. I hope the woman can tell us something about the former owners of the Main Street house. She's supposed to have been great friends with Catherine."

"She's also in her nineties," Viv frowned. "I hope she still has her mental faculties intact."

"We'll find out." Lin stood, rinsed her plate and mug in the sink, and placed them in the dishwasher. "I need to get to work or Leonard will get fussy."

"See you later."

Ninety-four-year old Elizabeth Hanes was slim, petite, and had silver-gray hair cut short with a fringe of bangs over her forehead. She was smart and articulate and the cousins needn't have been concerned about her mental state.

Wearing jeans and a short-sleeved white shirt, the woman greeted Lin and Viv at the front door with two Labradoodles by her side. "This is Yankee and this one is Dandy."

The cousins pet the dogs before heading out to the covered patio where there were plates of cookies and cut-up veggies with a dipping sauce. A pitcher of iced water and another one with lemonade sat on the rattan coffee table.

"Help yourself to refreshments," Elizabeth encouraged them.

The dogs went to play in the large rear yard being sure to stay away from the many flower gardens that dotted the edges of the lawn. The view of the gardens and the marsh in the distance was peaceful and calming.

"You have a lovely home," Viv told the woman.

"I've been out here in Tom Nevers for decades. I love this section of the island. I walk four miles a day, rain or shine. There are lots of places for a quiet walk nearby."

"I have a dog, too. He loves a good walk," Lin smiled.

"Do you live alone?" Viv asked the older woman.

"My daughter and her family live in the other side of the house. We cleverly split this place so that we each have our privacy. You'd never know from looking at the house that it's been made into a two-family. It worked out well for all of us. My daughter is a teacher and her husband is a firefighter. The prices of homes on the island are too high. They wouldn't have been able to stay here. I like having them next door. It's a win for me and them."

"Do you have grandkids?"

"I have four grandkids and four great-grandchildren." Elizabeth looked pleased.

"As I said when we spoke on the phone, we heard that you were good friends with Catherine Whittaker." Lin sipped from her glass of lemonade.

Elizabeth nodded. "Catherine and I were like sisters. I loved that woman. I'm so sorry she's gone. We had so many wonderful times together. Time marches on, I'm afraid."

"How did you meet?"

A warm smile spread over the older woman's

face. "We met in college. Can you believe that? Over seventy years ago. Catherine went on to study law and I became a mathematics professor. We were both ahead of our time. We both married and moved to Boston. We kept up our friendship. Eventually, we each bought second homes on the island. After I stopped teaching, I made this my permanent home. Catherine and her husband moved here about ten years before my husband and I did. My husband passed a few years ago. It was a difficult time, losing my husband and Catherine so close together."

Viv said, "We heard a rumor that the Whittakers believed there was a ghost in their house."

"There *was* a ghost in their house," Elizabeth said firmly. "He's probably still there."

"Did you experience seeing or hearing the spirit?" Lin leaned slightly forward.

"I could tell when he was around. The space would get freezing cold."

"Did he ever appear to the Whittakers?"

"You mean did they ever see him?"

Lin nodded.

"He never made himself visible to anyone." Elizabeth shook her head and looked out over the lawn at the two dogs romping with each other. "Sometimes, a door latch would open, or it would rattle incessantly. There was a missing drawer pull on one of Catherine's dressers. She spoke to her husband how it bothered her that the pull couldn't be found." The woman's eyes brightened. "Guess what appeared on her dresser later that day?"

"The drawer pull." Viv grinned.

"That's right."

"The ghost was always amiable?" Lin asked.

"Always. He could be mischievous, moving Catherine's reading glasses to another table, hiding Nicholas's pipe, things like that. Catherine never told me he was anything but playful and pleasant."

Lin and Viv shared a look. That wasn't how the ghost had been behaving recently.

"Why do you want to know about the ghost?" Elizabeth held the young women's gaze. "Are you skeptics?"

"Not at all. My husband has been hired to do a restoration on the Whittakers' former house. My husband told us there's a ghost who lives there. The ghost seems upset that the former owners are gone. He's in a poor state right now."

"I'm sorry to hear that." Elizabeth looked sad. "That's what Catherine called him. The Poor One."

"Why though? You told us the ghost was always

in good spirits when they lived there," Viv asked for clarification. "Why did she call him that?"

"Catherine believed the ghost was a servant who once lived and worked in that house," Elizabeth told them. "She was sure that the servant was killed in the house."

"Killed? Who would have killed him?" Lin looked surprised at this piece of news.

"Catherine only told me that the ghost was a servant who had been murdered. She never told me who the killer was or why the Poor One died. I don't know if she knew."

"Did Catherine know the servant's name?"

"I don't believe she did. She always referred to him as the Poor One."

"Did she have a guess as to when he died?"

"She suspected it might be in the mid-1800s. Her ancestor George Bean owned the house back then. He was a poor excuse for a human being as far as Catherine knew. She'd done some research on her ancestors and discovered what a foul person Mr. Bean was. A cheat and a liar, the man was a crude, money-grubbing, power-hungry devil. Any account of the man from the past reported the same things. Catherine was sorry to call him her ancestor. It upset her to have such a terrible person in her family tree. Maybe George Bean had something to do with the servant's untimely death. But really? Who knows? There were other scoundrels and crooks in Catherine's family. My friend was a saint. She wanted children so badly, but it was not to be. She was an extremely generous person. She and her husband Nicholas donated millions of dollars to charities, universities, foundations. It was her wish to make things better for people. I think it was a way of atoning for the sins of her ancestors."

"She sounds like a lovely person," Viv said.

"She was a dear, kind, loving woman. I was lucky to have known her."

Yankee and Dandy bounced over to the three women sitting around the coffee table, and the well-mannered dogs received pats and scratches behind their ears before trotting off to the side of the house.

"Such good dogs." Lin watched them go.

"They're always having fun together. They're the best of pals. Maybe I should have named them Catherine and Elizabeth." The older woman looked wistful.

Back in the car on the road to town, Lin said, "We made some headway. Elizabeth was helpful."

"We learned that the Poor One was probably killed in the Main Street house by an ancestor of

Catherine Whittaker. That must be why he's always angry."

"But," Lin pointed out, "he wasn't angry at all when Catherine and her husband lived in the house."

"So why is he in such a rage now?" Viv watched the road as they drove along.

"He misses Catherine and Nicholas?"

"Wouldn't missing someone make you feel mostly sad, not angry?"

"Well, maybe he doesn't like the new owners?" Lin surmised.

"Let's ask him when we go there tomorrow evening," Viv suggested. "Do you think what you felt on the dock at the inner harbor is a link to the Poor One?"

Lin didn't answer for a few seconds, then she took in a long breath. "I most certainly do."

22

The Mailman didn't show up on the night John and Jeff kept watch outside April's apartment house and he was absent again when the Blakes sat out all night hoping to see him. Lin had wished he would appear on one of the nights since he wrote in his last note that he would be back very soon. She and Jeff would keep watch later that evening.

She said to Viv, "I wonder if the Mailman knows our vehicles and that's why he hasn't dropped off a new note."

"I'd bet he does. He's devious and clever. A week ago we suspected someone was following us home from town. It must have been him. He knows where I live and what I drive. I'm certain he knows where you live, too." Viv's face hardened. "It makes me so angry that he can harass people for so many years and get away with it."

"If we have anything to say about it," Lin replied, "then he's going to get caught very soon."

"Do you sense that or is it wishful thinking?"

"It's wishful thinking," Lin sighed.

"Darn."

As the cousins headed up the walkway to the Blakes's house to meet April, she came around the corner.

April looked tired and down. "I'm getting really tired of this. I just want to live a normal life."

"We'll be so happy when that day comes," Viv told her.

The young women planned to walk around the neighborhood and discuss any possibility that someone on the street could be the culprit.

"We talked to the church organist, Bill Barre," Lin said. "He told us he used to live in the neighborhood."

"Yeah, he did. He moved into town a few years ago."

"He told us his hip bothered him and that he wanted to be closer to stores and restaurants."

"Really? I don't think it was a hip issue that prompted him to move," April said.

"No?" Lin looked at her with a quizzical expression.

"My father would never tell you this so don't bring it up with him, but Mr. Barre stole some tools from him and my dad was furious. The tools were brand new and he left them in the front yard one day. When he came out, they were gone. A week later, he stopped to chat with Mr. Barre and he saw his tools in Barre's driveway. Dad couldn't believe it, he confronted him, but Barre said he didn't know what Dad was talking about. He got all indignant and wouldn't speak to my father anymore. Dad was sure the tools were his. It's weird, isn't it?"

Lin's eyes had gone wide. "When did this happen?"

"It was the same year the notes started, but the notes had been arriving for months before Mr. Barre stole the tools so he didn't start sending the notes to get back at my dad for accusing him," April said.

"Some people get a thrill from stealing things," Viv said. "It happens in my bookstore. People who have plenty of money, steal a couple of books. It's not because they can't afford the things. It's because of the rush they get when they get away with it."

They continued their walk along the street with

April telling them who lived in the houses as they passed by.

"I wouldn't suspect any one of the people who live here. About five of the houses have changed hands over the years so the residents weren't living here at the time the notes started."

They walked into the next neighborhood along a connecting road and April pointed out the houses where she knew the people.

"I don't know the people well. I've just run into them in town or at events."

They strolled by a big yellow Colonial house with pretty landscaping.

"My parents used to be friendly with the couple who lived there."

"Did they move away?" Viv asked.

"They sold the house not long ago and bought another place, but the friendship dried up before that. I asked Mom and Dad why they didn't get together with them anymore, and Dad just said that they and the other couple were never free at the same time. My sisters and I always thought something else had happened and our parents didn't want to get into it with us." April shrugged.

"Who was the couple?" Lin asked.

"Michael and Eileen Salem. Do you know them?

They bought an antique house on upper Main Street."

Lin was surprised to hear the comments about April's parents and the Salems. "We do know them. Jeff's company has been hired to do the restoration of their house."

"Small world," Viv said.

"Yeah, and an island is even smaller. A lot of people know each other here," April said. "You can't help but run into other residents. There are only two grocery stores, one elementary school, one middle and one high school, and one hospital. People are bound to bump into each other."

"Do you remember when your parents and the Salems stopped getting together?" Lin questioned.

"Oh, it was a long time ago. I don't remember exactly."

After walking through the neighborhoods, April went to her workshop and Lin and Viv strolled back to Viv's house.

"So Bill Barre stole some things from Jim Blake," Viv brought up the odd happening. "Next time Bill comes into the bookstore, I'll be sure to keep my eye on him since he seems to have a case of sticky fingers. I don't need him lifting any of my merchandise."

"And the Blakes used to be friendly with the Salems," Lin pointed out. "I wonder what happened to cool the friendship."

"The Salems aren't permanent residents. Maybe it just fizzled out. It happens."

Jeff had to work later than planned so Lin told him to drive over to April's place when he finished and she'd meet him there. She told him to be sure to text her when he was done.

Lin decided to walk over to the Main Street house to visit the ghost. When Jeff called, it would only take her ten minutes to walk to April's street. She wasn't looking forward to spending another night in a vehicle waiting for the Mailman to show up, but she knew it had to be done.

She put the key in the lock and entered the big antique home, switched on the lights, and went upstairs to the bedroom where the old desk stood by the windows.

Since that was the only piece of furniture left in the room, Lin slid down to sit on the floor with her back resting against the wall.

"I'm here," she said softly to the ghost. "I'm

feeling worn out at the moment. I have two things I'm looking into and I don't feel like I'm making any headway with either one."

There was no response.

Lin looked out the window at the waning light of the day.

"I heard that Catherine called you the Poor One."

Everything remained quiet.

"We talked to Catherine's friend Elizabeth Hanes. She told us that you seemed to be happy here with Catherine and Nicholas. Elizabeth loved her friendship with Catherine. She said they were like sisters. Catherine told Elizabeth that she thought you were murdered. She didn't know by whom, or when or why it happened."

Lin felt the temperature in the room drop by at least twenty degrees. She knew the ghost was listening to her.

"You must know this house was built for George Bean in 1830. Catherine said he wasn't a very nice man. She was ashamed to have him as an ancestor. A long time ago, the Bean family owned land next to the inner harbor. I was there the other day. The current owner has a wooden dock there now. You have to walk down a short trail to reach it. When I stood on the dock, I felt like I was under the water. I tried to swim, but I couldn't lift my arms or kick my feet. It felt like I was sinking down in the cold dark water. It was terrifying."

Lin waited for a response, and then she thought she could see some shimmering particles near the desk. She stood and walked closer.

"Did you die in the inner harbor?" she asked softly.

The piece of paper materialized on the desk and the pen floated above it. Lin watched as it wobbled toward the paper. The tip pointed down and shakily hovered in the air, then the tip hit the paper with a *thump* and the pen dropped onto the desk.

Lin's heart skipped a beat. A word was written there.

No

Stunned, Lin blinked. "No? You weren't killed in the inner harbor?" She was sure the ghost had died there.

"Did someone kill you?"

Nothing. The pen lay where it was on the desk.

"I really want to help you. Sometimes, things from the past are hidden. I'm trying to pull away at the years to find out what happened to you, to find out what you want me to do."

Lin stared at the pen, wishing it would move again.

"Can you tell me your name? It would be so much help if I knew your name."

The pen shuddered, and Lin held her breath.

Rising from the desk, seemingly by itself, the pen shivered in the air, seemed to slip for a moment, and then hit the paper and fell onto the desk.

Lin peered at the paper.

A W

"A W? Are those your initials? They must be. Thank you." Some tears gathered in Lin's eyes. "That's so much help." She smiled. "I promise I'll find you. And I'll find out what you need from me."

23

After dinner, Lin and Viv went to visit Anton to do some research with him on the ghost. As usual, the man had tea, cold drinks, coffee, and a plate of cut-up fruit and some brownies to snack on.

When Anton welcomed the cousins, Nicky, and Queenie into his home, the dog and cat ran into the living room to sit on top of the sofa back so they could peer out the big window. Lin and Viv took seats at the huge kitchen table that was loaded with notebooks, books, and Anton's laptop.

"So," he started in right away. "You have the ghost's initials, A. W."

"I think so," Lin told him. "I asked his name and he wrote those two letters on the paper. They *must* be his initials."

"Good, good." Anton handed a hard cover book to Lin and one to Viv. "Those are collections of letters sent from island residents to friends and family from the 1800s to the early 1900s. It can be tedious work if you're looking for someone in particular, but I've had good luck finding things in those books. Some letters and correspondence from Nantucket natives can be found in research databases. I'll concentrate on those." He opened his laptop and began to tap the keys.

Lin said, "When I was in the Main Street house, I asked the ghost if he had died in the inner harbor."

Anton looked up.

"He wrote 'No' on the paper. I was sure the Linton-Campbells' dock had a connection to the ghost. Catherine Whittaker believed a young house servant had been murdered in her home years ago. She thought the servant was the ghost."

Anton adjusted his eyeglasses. "The dock may still have a connection to the ghost. He just didn't drown there. Didn't Libby say the person didn't die there? His body must have been tossed into the water."

"That's what I said." Viv turned a page of the book she had in front of her and studied the letters printed there.

The three researchers worked for two hours, sipping beverages, and occasionally taking some fruit or a brownie from the platter in the center of the table.

Leaning back in her chair, Lin stretched and yawned. "I haven't found one single thing."

"Keep looking," Viv encouraged. "It's only 10pm."

Needing a break, Lin told Anton what they'd learned about Bill Barre and the Salems when they met April the previous day.

"It's not that unusual for a person to be a klepto-maniac." Anton removed his glasses and rubbed his eyes. "It doesn't mean they're also a stalker."

"No, but doesn't it make you suspect Bill?" Viv questioned.

"It could, but we need to analyze things in a rational way. Perhaps Mr. Barre was angry with Jim Blake that day and decided to teach him a lesson by grabbing his tools."

"That's not something most people would do," Lin pointed out.

"It may have been the heat of the moment. Mr. Barre may have immediately regretted what he'd done, but didn't know how to return the items ... so he kept them and hoped he wouldn't be found out."

"But he had them right in his driveway. He was

using them when Jim Blake walked by and saw his new tools in Bill's yard." Viv sounded exasperated.

"We don't know the full circumstances," Anton defended his idea. "We don't know what Mr. Barre was thinking."

"He was thinking *I'm going to steal those tools*," Viv insisted. "It's out of the ordinary. A person's unusual behavior should be considered. He also lived in the Blakes' neighborhood when the notes started. I put him on the suspect list."

"I have to agree with Viv." Lin took a swallow of her coffee. "Bill Barre was also teaching at the high school when the Blake sisters were going there. I think Bill belongs on the list of suspects."

"Fine. I surrender." Anton let out a breath of air. "And what about the Salems? Are you putting them on the suspect list simply because they were once friendly with the Blakes and then the friendship faded?"

"When you put it that way," Viv smiled, "maybe not. It's too little to go on."

"The ghost seems to get upset when the Salems stop in at the Main Street house, but the Whittakers lived there for decades and now the house is being renovated. It's a lot of change. The ghost was used to things the way they were."

"I think the ghost will adjust in time." Anton returned to his laptop, and in fifteen minutes, he sat up. "I think I found him. Adam Winn. A.W. He's mentioned in this piece of correspondence."

"You found him?" Lin jumped from her seat to go around the table to look over the man's shoulder.

"Read it out loud?" Viv requested.

"It's written by a native of the island. She's writing about a social event she attended at the Main Street house. She talks about what a wonderful time everyone had, she tells about the food, some people who were present, and comments on the music that was played. She mentions a young house boy, Adam. She reports that he was a new employee of the Beans'. The writer says she found him to be quite good-looking and that he had a winning personality."

"When was the letter written?" Lin squinted at the laptop screen.

"1839."

"George Bean was living there then," Viv noted. "Who else lived there? George was married, wasn't he?"

Anton shuffled through his notebooks. "I know I could make a document on my laptop, but I prefer to use real paper and a pen," he headed off the cousins' usual suggestion to keep his notes in an online document. "Here it is. George Bean's wife was named Sybil. They had three daughters, Pollyanna, Rebecca, and Lilibeth."

"So they all must have lived in the house at the time?" Lin guessed.

"It doesn't say. George would have been in his early fifties in 1839," Anton calculated in his head. Sybil was ten years younger than George. They married when Sybil was twenty. If they had children right away, the daughters would have been in their late teens and very early twenties in 1839." He turned the notebook page. "I see here that a brother of George Bean lived two streets over and was a regular visitor to the house. The Beans were known to be frequent entertainers."

"Adam was either an island native or he may have come from the mainland." Lin paced around the kitchen. "The letter doesn't mention how old Adam was in 1839?"

"It doesn't. But the woman wrote that he was a *very young man*."

"A teen?" Viv asked.

"Probably," Anton said with a nod. "Possibly a late teen to twenty years of age, perhaps."

"This is great." Standing behind Anton's chair,

Lin wrapped her arms around his shoulders and gave him a hug, causing the man to blush. "Thank you so much. You always come through for us. I don't know what we'd do without you. I'd like to go to see the ghost. I want to tell him we know his name."

"It's late," Viv said. "You don't think anyone will call the cops on us if they see we're inside the house?"

"If they do, we'll just say we're there to help a ghost," Lin kept a straight face. "Do you want to come along with us?" she asked the historian.

"Oh, me?" Anton was surprised to be invited. "I don't know. Will my presence upset the spirit?"

"I'm going to tell the ghost you were the one who found his name." Lin cleared the table. "That will make him happy. You won't cause him any upset."

"I'd like to go along then. I would dearly love to see that pen in action." Anton stood. "Shall the dog and cat stay here?"

"They can come, too." Lin called Nicky and Queenie to join them, and they all left the house and headed for upper Main Street.

Inside the house's foyer, Anton turned in a circle admiring the woodwork and the staircase. "I've never been in this house. It's a very fine home. Worn around the edges, but Jeff and his team will take care of that and return the house to its former glory." He lowered his voice. "Where does the ghost reside?"

"Upstairs," Viv gestured.

The dog and cat moved from room to room, sniffing in every corner.

"It's very quiet in here," Anton noted. "No knocking, no noises at all."

"He's been less noisy," Lin explained. "Maybe that's a sign he's becoming more accepting of the changes taking place."

They climbed the stairs with Nicky and Queenie following, and when they reached the second floor, the pets darted right into the main bedroom where the ghost was usually found.

"They know he's here," Viv said.

"They always know," Lin nodded.

"There's the desk." Anton stood just inside the room. He didn't make a move to walk over to the antique piece of furniture.

Lin spoke. "We're here, Lin and Viv. And this is our friend, Anton, and we brought our cat and dog along, too."

Nicky and Queenie sat beside the desk looking up into the air. Nicky's tail was wagging and Queenie was purring.

After a minute, Lin could see some shimmering particles between the desk and the windows. "Anton helped us with the research to find out your name. The initials you gave me were a big help. Anton found an old letter that mentioned someone named Adam Winn. Is that you?"

Silence greeted the question and Lin was about to speak again, when they all saw the pen and paper appear. The pen floated in the air, then tapped the piece of paper and fell over.

Anton gasped. Nicky's tail wagged faster and Queenie trilled.

Lin moved forward and looked down at the paper.

Yes.

Lin's heart filled with joy. "You're Adam Winn. I'm so glad to know your name."

Anton moved closer and whispered, "Ask him if he was killed in this house."

Before Lin could say anything, the pen floated up and began to shudder, dip, and lift. It was like it was floating on a hurricane's air currents, so violently did it fall and rise. In a moment, it moved over the paper as if an invisible hand made it go.

"What's he writing?" Viv came up next to Anton.

"Nothing," Lin said softly. "The paper is blank."

They waited, but still nothing showed on the paper. The pen's movements became furious and maniacal.

"What's going on?" Anton's question was barely audible.

Knocking sounds could be heard against the room's four walls, along with ringing phones, and a terrible wail.

The pen smashed against the paper, and then rolled onto the desk. The sounds stopped.

"Thank heavens. Does it say anything?" Viv asked her cousin while clutching Anton's arm.

Lin's eyes widened, and she turned to her companions looking dumbfounded. "Yes. It says *April*."

24

Lin and Jeff worked in the kitchen preparing a dinner of vegetable lasagna, garlic bread, and salad when their guests, Viv and John came into the kitchen from the deck. Nicky and Queenie took off across the deck together and darted into the field behind the house.

"Those two." Viv chuckled at the two friends. "Don't get in their way. They're on a mission."

John placed a bottle of homemade dressing and an angel food cake with strawberries and whipped cream on the table.

"Can we eat the dessert before the dinner?" Jeff ogled the cake.

"You can do whatever you want," Viv assured

him as she put the bottle of homemade non-alcoholic sangria in the fridge.

"Don't tell him that," Lin warned. "Or it would be sweets all day, every day."

"It's true." Jeff owned up to his sweet tooth with a smile and went to get a knife from the drawer. "Maybe just one tiny slice."

Lin rolled her eyes. "I try to keep you healthy. Do what you must."

When the food was ready, they took seats around the long wooden kitchen table.

"Since it's so humid out, we thought it would be more comfortable to eat inside," Jeff explained as he served squares of lasagna to everyone.

"It's fine with me. I can't handle the humidity," John admitted.

"After we eat, come and see the second floor room. We just put a second coat of paint on the walls. It's looking really good. When the whole upstairs is done, the space is going to be used as a sitting room, but for now, Jeff is going to use it as his office."

"Great idea," Viv said as she used the tongs to put salad in her bowl. "One second floor space complete. Only four more to go."

"Thanks," Jeff said. "The whole thing will be

completed by the time we need to go to the old age home."

"You did the sitting room pretty fast." John poured sangria into the glasses.

Lin's jaw hung open for a second. "It took us a year."

"Oh." John shrugged. "That long? One room a year ... then the upstairs will be done in only four more years."

"Good thing it doesn't take that long to renovate a house for your clients," Viv giggled and then sipped her drink. "Oh, that's tasty," she told her husband. "I don't miss the alcohol one bit."

John gave a nod and a smile. "One of my many talents."

"That's why I married you," Viv said.

"I thought you married me because of my boat." John passed around the platter of garlic bread.

"That, too."

When dinner was done, they took mugs of coffee and the angel food cake outside to eat on the deck. Lin and Jeff had strung lights over the deck and they looked festive when he switched them on.

The cat and dog had eaten their dinners and were now napping on one of the lounge chairs on the stone patio.

Jeff and John had been told about the visit Lin, Viv, and Anton paid to the Main Street house the previous night.

John asked, "Why did the ghost write *April* on that piece of paper?"

Lin sipped her coffee. "He must know that she's being harassed."

"How would he know?" John added more strawberries to his plate.

Viv sighed. "He's a ghost, John."

"But he's stuck in that house all the time. He doesn't leave."

Jeff said, "He might be able to sense things."

"How though?" John asked.

"You know, like mental telepathy." Jeff shrugged.

"None of us knows how these things work," Lin admitted. "There's no explaining it, at least, not until we pass away ourselves."

"I'm in no rush to find out," John assured them. "So the ghost thinks April is in danger?"

They all looked at Lin.

"I guess he does."

"Just to be clear, I don't want anything to do with ghosts," John told them, "but it sure is pretty cool."

"Is there some way the ghost might be able to

help figure out who the Mailman is?" Jeff asked slicing a second helping of cake.

"It's a good question," Lin said. "I just don't know how he'd go about helping. Unless, I ask him if he knows who is harassing April and he writes a name on the paper."

"That would save us a lot of trouble," Viv said.

"If the ghost wrote down the Mailman's name, we'd know who it was, but we couldn't bring that information to the police," Jeff said. "*A ghost told us* wouldn't go over that well with them."

The others laughed.

"Well, if we knew who it was, we could keep an eye on him and catch him the next time he left a note for April," Lin pointed out.

"And April would know who to keep an eye out for and keep away from him if he approached," Viv explained.

"We'd have to make up some story to tell April about why we suspected him," Lin said, "but we could come up with something. I'll ask the ghost the next time I visit him. I've been thinking about the recent notes April has received." Lin used her napkin to dab some whipped cream from her lip. "Some of the letters have a unique slant to them. I wonder if we could get something handwritten by

Bill Barre to compare to the notes. We could see if his handwriting matches the words on the notes."

"That's a great idea." Viv's eyes sparkled. "But how would we go about getting a sample from him?"

"That's the problem," Lin admitted. "Any ideas?"

No one came up with anything.

"Think about it for a while. One of us will think of a way."

"We should get going to the beach," Jeff told them. "Or we'll miss the bands."

"I've been looking forward to this." Viv stood to clear away the plates. "I like the Boston band that's going to play."

While they cleaned up, they discussed the musical groups that would be playing on Jetties Beach that evening. Jeff and John went out to load beach chairs into the Jeep while Lin and Viv put the food away.

Lin went out to the patio. "Are you two going to stay outside while we're gone?" she asked the cat and dog.

They looked up at her with sleepy eyes.

"I'm leaving the doggy door open if you want to go into the house. We won't be late. Guard the house," she told the animals even though she knew they'd be sound asleep by the time she was back in the kitchen.

John parked the Jeep in the big lot at the beach and they all got out and walked down to the sand where they found Leonard and Heather, and their friends the Snow family. The beach restaurant's outdoor seating was full and the beach was busy with groups of people mingling and chatting. After setting up their chairs next to the others, they played some beach games together before the bands would begin the show.

Lin and Viv went up to the restaurant to use the bathroom and get some drinks and on the way back, they ran into Eileen and Michael Salem.

"What a great turnout," Michael said after greeting the cousins.

"I saw a couple of these bands in Boston a year ago," Eileen told them. "They're really great."

Leonard, Jeff, John, and the Snows came over to say hello and chat.

"There's good progress on the house," Michael told Jeff. "We stop there most evenings to have a look at what's been done."

"We love how things are turning out," Eileen said. "We're very pleased to have hired your company."

Jeff thanked them and told them what to expect over the next week to ten days. "It's a long process, but it will be well worth it."

While the others conversed, Eileen sidled up to Lin. "We went to the house the other night and the ghost was having a fit."

"Was he? I thought things were improving."

"They're not." Eileen's cheeks turned red with annoyance. "Can you do anything about it?"

"These things can go very slowly," Lin informed the woman. "The spirit moves at its own pace. It can't be rushed, but the outcome is usually favorable."

"It better be. I'm losing my patience. What does he want?"

"I'm unsure," Lin admitted.

"What does who want?" Michael came over to join them.

"We're talking about our resident *guest*," Eileen muttered.

"He was quite wound up when we were there the other night," Michael shared.

"I think he's starting to calm down," Lin told the couple. "Things will improve soon. He just needs to get to know you."

"Does he have to stay?" Eileen questioned.

"Could you convince him to move into a different house?"

"He has a connection to your house. He wouldn't want to go elsewhere," Lin explained and then tried to change the subject. "Where did you say you were staying while the Main Street house is being restored?"

"We rented a house. We sold the home we'd owned for years." Eileen sniffed and took some deep breaths. The discussion about the ghost had clearly upset her.

"Is the rental in town?"

"It's close to town," Michael said. "Walking distance. It's off the Madaket Road. It's hard to be in a rental. Our own things are in storage. It will be nice to get our own things into the new house so we can settle in."

"Yes, I understand. We're building a second floor to our home and the work has been going on for a year. It can be tiring to live with a building project. Viv and I are friendly with Julie and April Blake. You know the Blakes, right?"

"We do." Michael seemed to take on a more formal posture. "They're nice people. Julie and her sisters are very pleasant young women."

"Do you see the Blakes much?"

"We don't. We'd better go take our seats. The show will be starting soon." Michael turned to his wife who was talking with Viv and the Snows. "Why don't we sit down now," he said to her before waving to the others. "Nice to chat with you."

Michael took Eileen's arm and they hurried away.

Viv came over to her cousin. "The Salems left kind of abruptly. Did you say something to make Michael want to hurry away?"

"I must have, but I'm not sure what it was."

25

Lin was outside watering the flower pots while Nicky sniffed around the patio when the dog's head snapped up and he trotted around to the side yard. Wondering what caught his attention, she set down the watering can, wiped her hands on her jean shorts, and walked around the house to find Nicky wagging his little tail at Anton.

"Hey," Lin called to the man. "Come for a visit?"

"Not exactly a visit." Anton carried a briefcase and laptop bag. "Are you busy? Can you spare a few moments?"

"I'm not busy. I just got home from work and was watering the flowers. Jeff's working late, as usual. Want something to drink?" They walked together to the backyard and stepped up onto the deck.

"Jeff needs to hire another crew before he and Kurt run themselves into the ground," Anton said.

Nicky woofed.

"See, the dog agrees with me." Anton and Lin went into the kitchen and she took a pitcher of iced tea from the fridge. "Want a glass?"

"I'd love a glass. I'm parched. I haven't had time today to even have lunch." He sat at the kitchen island and opened his briefcase.

"We had lasagna last night and there are tons of leftovers. I'll heat up a plate for you."

Anton sighed. "I knew coming here was a good idea."

Lin laughed and placed a square of lasagna on a plate and heated it in the microwave. While it warmed, she made a small salad and brought the bowl and a fork to Anton. "Here's some of John's homemade dressing. It's delish." She went back to get his meal and a glass of iced tea.

"Wonderful." Anton took a bite. "Is this dinner or lunch?"

"It can be whatever you want it to be." Lin sat down on the stool next to the man. "Why have you been so busy today?"

Anton shook his head. "I had an online meeting with a publisher about a new book, I had a meeting at the historical library, I gave a short lecture on Nantucket history at the Whaling Museum, met Libby in 'Sconset to see a friend, and I did some research. Which is why I'm here."

"Did you find something about our ghost?" Lin looked eagerly at the historian.

"I did. I knew I'd find some things, but *when* was the question." Anton finished off the lasagna and the salad, and then took a long swig of his iced tea. "That was delicious."

"There's also some angel food cake and whipped cream, if you'd like some."

"Oh dear, is there? I can't say no to angel food cake. It's one of my favorites. Just a small piece or I'll be ten pounds heavier than when I arrived here."

Lin smiled and brought over a dessert plate with the cake, some strawberries, and cream.

"Can you tell me what you found?"

Anton swallowed. "I found a treasure trove of a database that will be useful for the future. It was also useful for the present case you're working on. The database contains documents from the seventeen and eighteen hundreds with many letters written by ordinary people. I find old letters to be the most informative. They shed light on the times like nothing else can. Reading old letters makes the past come alive. Anyway, I digress." He placed his dessert fork on the plate and reached for his laptop. "I saved the document in my files." He tapped away until he found what he was looking for.

Turning the laptop so Lin could better see, he said, "Here it is. It's handwritten which can be hard to decipher. Look here." He pointed to the middle part of the letter written in the 1830s. "The person who wrote the letter is a friend of one of George Bean's daughters. She writes that a new house boy is sweet on Lilibeth Bean. And, Lilibeth was sweet on the house boy... whose name just happens to be Adam Winn."

Lin leaned closer to read the letter. "Wow. Lilibeth and Adam had feelings for each other. I bet that didn't go over too well with Mr. and Mrs. Bean. No way would they have allowed one of their daughters to date a servant." She sat up and turned to Anton. "Do you think Adam got fired?"

"If he did," Anton said, "Catherine Whittaker would have been wrong about the young man having died in the Main Street house."

Lin's expression turned to one of alarm. "What if Adam was forbidden to see Lilibeth, but returned to the Bean's home, and got caught there?"

Anton's eyebrows rose up his forehead. "Oh, no."

"George Bean might have been the one who killed Adam."

"Should you go talk to the ghost?" Anton asked. "Maybe that's the reason he is always so upset."

Lin was about to nod, but stopped. "I think that's the reason Adam remains in the house. But I don't think that's the reason he's so upset. The Whittakers told friends the ghost was calm, quiet, though at times, mischievous. That doesn't sound like the spirit we've come to know."

"Then it must be because the Whittakers passed away," Anton guessed.

"And because there are new owners and the house is being restored and renovated." She stood. "Want to come with me?"

"I'll join you, yes."

The work crews were gone for the day by the time Lin, Anton, and Nicky arrived at the Main Street house, and Lin used the spare key to let them inside. They climbed the stairs and went into the main bedroom, and to Lin's surprise, Sebastian and Emily stood shimmering by the windows.

"Oh," she said in surprise.

"What is it?" Anton looked around the room to find the source of the young woman's gasp.

Wagging his tail, the dog trotted over to the other side of the room.

"It's Emily and Sebastian."

"They're here? Where?" Anton asked.

"By the windows."

"I'm honored to be in their presence." Anton nodded in their direction, and then whispered, "But why are they here?"

Lin shrugged. "When they appear to me, it's usually because they're trying to tell me something. I'm going to clear my mind and try to sense a message from them." She took in deep breaths and attempted to empty her mind of thoughts, ideas, and worries.

Images flashed behind her eyes. A pen moving in the air, pieces of papers floating on the breeze, a note left by the Mailman ... the letters on the page beginning to swirl. Faster and faster the letters unformed and turned into little scratches and lines, and then reformed into words. The image kept on like that for almost a full minute before fading away.

Lin took a quick step back and looked to the windows. Her ancestors were gone.

Nicky whined and lay down on the floor.

"Are you all right?" Anton touched Lin's arm.

She nodded and touched her forehead. "I'm

okay. I saw the notes the Mailman left for April. The words on the paper kept twisting around and reforming. I don't know what it means." Lin noticed the pen and paper had appeared on the antique desk.

"Adam? Are you here?"

She got no response. "Adam, Anton found a letter from long ago. It was written by a friend of Lilibeth. The letter said that you and Lilibeth had feelings for one another."

Suddenly, knocking sounded on the walls and got louder and louder. Noises of furniture being pushed over the floor filled the air. A pitiful wail hurt Lin's eardrums.

"What's going on?" Anton clamped his hands over his ears.

"What I said must have touched a nerve." Lin had to raise her voice to be heard.

The point of the pen on the table pounded at the piece of paper on the desk and Lin walked closer to see, but when she was near the windows, she saw a van pulling to the side of the street in front of the house.

"The Salems are here. Eileen is not going to be happy about all the noise the ghost is making."

"Shall we go downstairs?" Anton asked.

"They'll come up. They know I'm here because the lights are on." Lin glanced at the paper to see one word written on it.

April

She really wanted to try to communicate with Adam and wished the Salems hadn't shown up until later. There were so many things she wanted to speak with the ghost about.

The couple's footsteps could be heard on the staircase, and in a few seconds they were in the room.

"What an ungodly racket." Eileen put her fingers in her ears to block out some of the noise.

"Have you been able to make any headway?" Michael questioned. "Do you know what's making him cause this racket?"

"Not exactly," Lin told them. "I guess it's just a bad day."

"We came to take a small table from one of the other bedrooms," Michael said. "The workers will be starting renovations up here soon. We want to look around at what was done today."

"I don't know how long we'll be here." Eileen frowned. "This is just too much."

"We'd better get going," Lin said. "I think the

noise will calm down soon." She took a quick look at the desk and saw that the paper and pen were gone.

Anton, Lin, and Nicky left the house and it was a relief to be outside away from the noise.

"I know it's their house, but the Salems seem to arrive at the most inopportune times. I was hoping to get more from the ghost."

"That's the second time he's written *April* on the paper," Anton noted.

"Yes," Lin said. "It worries me. We need to come up with some ideas ... and fast."

26

Back at home, Lin sat at the kitchen table with her chin in her hand, thinking. The ghost had written April's name on the paper twice. He didn't seem as interested in his own situation as he was in what was going on with April. That sent chills down Lin's back. The Mailman must be getting ready to escalate his harassment. That must be why Sebastian and Emily appeared in the Main Street house. They must be warning her.

Lin massaged the back of her neck and tried to recall the details of the vision her ancestors sent her. A pen, a piece of paper ... words lifting from the paper, twisting in the air, breaking apart, and then coming back together again.

She stood up so fast that she woke the dog. He barked in confusion.

"Sorry, Nick. Go back to sleep." Lin took her phone from the table and scrolled through her photos. "Here they are." She pulled up the two photos she'd taken of the last two notes April had received. Usually, they were printed messages, but these last two were handwritten.

Lin touched the screen to make the words larger. She studied the formations of the letters. Then she looked up, and her heart rate increased.

Michael Salem had been evasive when Lin spoke with him at the Jettie's Beach concert. The ghost's behavior was always much worse whenever Michael was in the house. The ghost is concerned about April. Michael and Eileen had once been friendly with the Blakes, but the friendship had faded. They used to live close to the Blakes, and now their rental house was within walking distance of the Blakes' residence, and of April's apartment house.

Is Michael Salem the Mailman? How can I get a sample of his handwriting?

An idea popped into Lin's head and she texted Jeff. The Salems must have signed a contract with Jeff and Kurt to restore and renovate their new house. She could use the contract signature to compare to the handwritten notes.

Jeff replied. *The contract is in the business office. I can swing by to pick them up after we finish here. Should be done in a couple of hours.*

The doorbell rang causing Lin to jump. Nicky leapt to his feet and barked twice before hurrying to the front door.

After looking through the peephole on the door, Lin opened it to find Jim Blake standing there.

"Lin, hi. I was driving home and decided to stop. I should have called first, but I was passing your street when I got the idea to come by. Do you have a few minutes?"

"Yes, sure." She opened the door wider for the man. "How about a drink? Some coffee? Tea?"

"Nothing, thanks. I don't want to take up your time."

Lin led him into the kitchen where they took seats at the table.

"What's on your mind? Is everything okay?" Lin studied Jim's face for a clue to what might be wrong.

"Everything's okay. April's okay." He ran his hand over his face. "I'm worried about her though. Things seem to be getting worse. The notes are more frequent. There are veiled threats in the notes. We honestly don't know what to do. Leah and I have been talking about taking April and leaving the island. We've had enough. We're thinking of selling our business and our properties." Jim looked into Lin's eyes. "You don't think the Mailman would follow us, do you?"

Lin blinked a few times, considering what he'd just told her. "I don't know. I don't think he would, but he clearly has some issues so who knows? He could track you down, but maybe, it would be too difficult for him to move away. Maybe he'd turn his attention to someone else. That's a terrible alternative. The solution would be to find out who he is."

"We've been trying to figure that out for years." Jim's eyes focused on the tabletop. "We're about to give up. We're trying to talk April into leaving here immediately. She could stay with one of her sisters. She's reluctant to leave. But I think she needs to get off the island and go someplace safe."

"I understand. Things can seem hopeless. It might be a good idea for April to go to the mainland for a while. It's a huge move for Leah and you to leave behind all you've built, your home, your friends."

"It is, but our daughters' safety is the only thing that matters." Jim's eyes looked moist.

"I know I've asked you before, but is there anything in the past that might have triggered someone to start sending the notes?" Lin questioned the man hoping to spark a memory.

"I've lain awake more nights than I care to admit going over and over any little thing I can think of. I always feel like it was someone at the school, a teacher, a coach, someone at church. Someone who had interactions with the girls. But I can't point my finger to anyone in particular."

"I heard you used to be friendly with the Salems. They lived around the block from you."

Jim looked at Lin. "Where did you hear that?"

"From April. Your friendship sort of faded?"

A muscle along Jim's jawline twitched. "You could say that."

"What happened? Was there a falling out?" Lin could see that the man had become more tense. A flash of anger showed in his eyes.

"Yeah, a falling out." Jim rubbed at the knuckles on his hand.

"Were you in business together?" Lin tried to get the man talking.

"We were not." Jim swallowed hard. "Maybe I'll take that drink you offered earlier. Do you happen to have a beer?"

"Sure. We have a few brands." Lin stood and went to the refrigerator where she looked to see what was in there. She told Jim what they had, and when he made his choice, Lin carried the bottle, a bottle opener, and a beer glass back to the table.

Jim opened the bottle and poured the amber-colored liquid into the glass. He took a long swallow. "We don't talk to the Salems anymore. We used to have a good time together. But all that stopped abruptly."

Lin listened without interrupting with questions, and when Jim stopped talking, she waited quietly for him to go on.

"We were close. Too close." Jim drank from his glass. "Michael and Leah had an affair."

Lin's jaw almost dropped. She didn't know what she was expecting, but that wasn't it. "Oh, no."

Jim nodded and took in a deep breath. "It went on for about six months. I caught them together. I stormed out of the house and went straight to the Salems' house to tell Eileen. It was a stupid thing to do, but my mind was blazing with rage and betrayal. Eileen was furious. She left me in their house and practically ran to our house. When she got there, she ranted and raved at Leah like a madwoman. Michael had already left before Eileen arrived. None of us ever wanted to see each other again. It was strained between me and Leah for at least a year afterwards. Neither one of us wanted to hurt our girls so we decided to stay together."

"Eileen and Michael stayed together, too. She must have forgiven him."

"I think Eileen probably held a grudge. She told Leah previously that Michael made her sign a prenuptial agreement before they got married. Eileen made good money as a lawyer, but Michael had inherited a bundle and she mustn't have wanted to lose out on the lifestyle they lived."

Lin nodded in understanding. She didn't want to bring up her suspicion that Michael might be the Mailman. She needed some proof before sharing her thoughts with the Blakes so she stayed mum. When Jeff got home with the contract, she'd analyze Michael's handwriting and compare it to the notes April had received.

"I'm sorry this happened. What a mess it must have been."

"We never told our daughters. They know nothing about the affair." Jim kept his hand wrapped around his beer mug. "I don't like talking about it. It opens old wounds. I try not to think about it. We avoid the Salems at all costs." He took another drink.

"Leah told me that Michael kept contacting her after I discovered the affair. He wanted her to go away with him. He even told Eileen that he was in love with Leah and that it might be better to dissolve their marriage. Leah repeatedly told him no. She didn't want to lose the girls. Finally, Michael gave up and stayed with Eileen. There were some rumors that Michael might want to run for public office and not divorcing Eileen would play out for the best. I'm only telling you because you asked about the Salems. This has nothing to do with the notes. Michael wouldn't do anything so stupid as to jeopardize his career."

"Did you suspect him?"

"For about a half-second. It's not Michael. He's too self-centered and self-absorbed. I'd better go. I just wanted you to know that we might be leaving the island. Thanks for the beer."

Feeling low, Lin walked Jim to the door and said goodbye.

27

She'd just been sitting on the sofa for ten minutes when the doorbell rang again and Lin and the dog looked at one another before going to see who was at the door.

"Who is it this time?" Lin asked aloud as she once again looked through the peephole. "It's Anton," she told the dog as she unlocked the door and opened it.

"Lin." Anton bustled inside, bent to pat Nicky, and walked quickly to the kitchen. "I found something important about the ghost." He placed his laptop on the kitchen island and opened it. "You have to see this."

Peering over the historian's shoulder, Lin

watched him tap at the keys until he was in an historical database.

"Here it is." Anton pointed to the screen. "It's a letter written by Lilibeth Bean when she was in her sixties and in poor health. It's addressed to her older sister Rebecca. Shortly after writing the letter, Lilibeth passed away."

"What does she write? Why is it important?"

Anton summarized, "She tells her sister that she has carried a secret for most of her life. Their father George discovered the romance between Lilibeth and Adam Winn, the house boy. George fired the young man and told him never to return to the house. But Adam Winn did return to see Lilibeth, and when George and his brother discovered the young man, tempers raged, and they killed Adam. The two removed the body, placed weights on it, and dumped it in the inner harbor in the Shawkemo area of the island. George found out that Lilibeth knew what they'd done and threatened her to remain silent. He sent her to Boston to live with an aunt and told her never to return to the island."

Anton paused, shook his head, and looked at Lin. "A father committed murder and threatened his own daughter. Shameful is too weak a word to describe this man." He sighed and went on. "Lilibeth told her sister that her health was failing and that she had to share what she knew before going to her grave. She wasn't unhappy about departing this world. She hoped to reunite with Adam in the next world. Lilibeth never married. She remained single her entire life."

Lin sank onto one of the kitchen stools. "What a sad and terrible story."

"Do you think that she and Adam were able to reunite?" Anton asked.

"I don't think so since Adam continues to stay in the Main Street house."

"Why wouldn't they reunite after death?"

"They probably can't find each other. It happens. I'll tell Adam about this letter when I go there. I had another visitor right before you. Jim Blake came to talk with me." Lin reported the conversation with Jim to Anton.

"Well, this is an interesting twist." The historian removed his glasses and wiped them with a small piece of cloth he kept in his pocket. "When will Jeff be home with the contract? I would bet a good amount of money that the contract signature will match the handwriting on the recent notes April has received."

"I hope so. This could be the break we've been

hoping for. I'm going to text April to see if she's at home. I want to go over to her place and tell her what we think about Michael Salem." Lin's fingers flew over her phone and in seconds, she received a response.

"I'm walking home right now. I'll be there in ten minutes. What's up?"

Lin sent a short text telling April that they had a good idea who the Mailman is and asked if she could come to see April in about thirty minutes.

"I'll go with you," Anton told the young woman.

"I'd like that, then we can stop by the Main Street house to speak to the ghost." Lin sent another text. "I'm telling Jeff where we're going."

Anton packed his laptop into the briefcase.

"April hasn't answered me." Lin stared at her phone. "The text indicates that she hasn't read it yet. It just says *delivered.*"

"She's probably talking to someone else."

The doorbell rang for the third time.

Lin said, "It's like New York's Grand Central Station in here tonight." She, Anton, and Nicky hurried to see who it was.

"It's Leonard." Lin's voice held a tone of surprise. She opened the door. "Hey."

"Hey, yourself." Leonard's brow furrowed. "Are you all right?"

"Yeah. Anton just came by a few minutes ago to tell me something about the new ghost." Lin's eyes narrowed. "Why are you asking?"

"I've had an awful feeling ever since I got home from work. I made dinner and read my book, but I couldn't shake the feeling that something was wrong with you."

Anton teased, "Well, we all know something is wrong with Carolin, but there isn't anything new."

Leonard chuckled. "I didn't bother texting or calling because if something *was* wrong, then I thought driving right over here would save time."

Lin reached out and touched his arm. "Thank you. I appreciate it. Come in. We're just getting ready to head over to April's." The young woman stopped short and wheeled around to face Leonard, her heart sinking. "I texted April, but she hasn't answered me."

Leonard's expression filled with worry. "Let's go."

"Where?" Anton was confused.

"To April's. If Leonard senses something is wrong, then something is wrong." Lin grabbed her small purse and keys and the three people and the dog dashed for the man's truck.

Lin and Nicky jumped into the rear seat while Anton took the front passenger seat.

Leonard started the engine. "Call April."

Lin sent the call, but it just rang and rang. "She's not picking up." She told Leonard her suspicions about Michael Salem.

"That's quite a story." Leonard turned the truck so abruptly that it careened around the corner in the moonless night. Lin grabbed hold of the dog and Anton pressed his hand against the dashboard.

"If you kill us, we won't be able to protect April," Anton warned the driver.

"Let's park at the end of her road and walk up the sidewalk," Lin suggested. "If we go roaring up to the house, it might alert Michael that we're on to him … if he's here."

"Or we'll go sneaking up and look in April's windows and discover she has a gentleman friend over." Anton rolled his eyes. "We don't know for sure that something is wrong."

"Yes, we do. I feel it." Leonard parked along the side of the street.

"Should we call the police?" Anton worried.

"What would we say? We think our friend is in danger because she isn't answering her phone?"

Leonard opened the truck door and stepped onto the quiet road.

Lin lifted Nicky out of the truck and set him on the ground and Anton slipped out of the front passenger seat.

"Why don't I go up to the house by myself. I can sneak around the side of the house and try to see inside. If we all go up together and Michael is inside with April, he might panic and do something stupid."

"Okay," Leonard told her reluctantly. "Anton and I will go stand across the street from the house. We'll crouch behind the parked cars there."

Lin felt her phone vibrate in her pocket and she grabbed it. "It's a text from Jeff. He says he and Kurt just stopped at a pub to drop off some paperwork for a reno on the place. Michael Salem was having a drink at the bar with a friend." She looked up at her friends with a look of bewilderment.

"So Michael isn't here after all," Anton said.

"But it has to be Michael." Lin stared at the ground, her mind going a mile a minute. "Our ghost gets upset every time Michael shows up at the Main Street house." A half-second later, she looked up, her eyes wide with realization. "Oh, no, no. I've warned April away from the wrong person."

"Then who..." Leonard stopped. "It's Eileen."

"Eileen Salem?" Anton seemed unable to take it all in. "Oh, dear."

Lin's finger jabbed at her phone screen sending a text to her husband asking if Eileen was with Michael at the pub."

The answer came back right away. *"No."*

"Let's go." Lin turned to look at the house where April lived. "Anton will go to the front door and ring the bell. I'll go to the side of the house and try to see inside. If I see Eileen with April, then I'll try to cause a diversion. But first I'll text you about what I see. Leonard can go to the rear of the house. There's a back porch there with a door to the rear hallway. If you hear me shout, then break in. Anton, then you call the police and tell them to get here fast."

"It's a plan." Anton walked along the sidewalk to the front porch of the house while Nicky and Lin hurried in the shadows to the side yard, and Leonard moved quietly to the rear of the property.

"Keep quiet, Nick," Lin whispered. She moved back to the tree line to get a better view. The lights were on inside and she could see someone standing in the living room. When the figure moved into the light, she could see it was Eileen Salem, and her heart dropped.

She sent a text to Anton and Leonard. *"Eileen is inside. Anton, in thirty seconds, ring the doorbell, then call the police and keep ringing that bell. Leonard, charge into the house as soon as you hear a shout or a crash. I don't see April."*

In the darkness, Lin searched the yard for a rock, but instead, found a loose brick on the back walkway that was of the right size and heft. Clutching it in her hand, she moved closer to the living room window, and then leaning back a little, she took two fast steps forward, moved her arm back at the same time, and then swung and released the brick.

To her amazement, it shattered the window and went sailing into the living room, and then she and the dog took off for the back of the house to follow Leonard into April's apartment.

When he heard the sound of smashing glass, Leonard kicked the back door in, charged down the hall, and then smashed the door with his shoulder a few times to break into April's apartment.

Lin and Nicky were right on his heels and the three of them raced into the place together. April was gagged and bound and was lying on the floor.

Eileen wheeled around toward the unexpected

and unwanted guests ... and then she lifted her hand and pointed a gun at them.

"Eileen, put the gun down. The police are coming. You don't have to do this," Lin pleaded.

Eileen's face hardened. "I do have to do this. I wasn't going to kill her here. I was taking her to the Cliffs. But you stupid people had to interfere, and now, you leave me no choice." The woman swiveled on her heel and aimed the gun at April.

Before she could pull the trigger, Nicky lunged at the woman, leapt into the air, and bit onto the wrist that held the gun.

Leonard rushed forward and tackled Eileen to the ground. The gun went off with a bang, but the bullet went into the wall.

Racing to April, Lin helped her to her feet. Leonard had Eileen's arms pulled behind her back and was kneeling on her while the woman wailed and screeched.

"Are you all right?" Lin pulled the taped gag off April's mouth.

Gasping, April leaned forward to catch her breath. "I'm okay ... now."

In minutes, the police rushed into the apartment with Anton right behind them.

"Thank the heavens." The historian leaned back

against the wall, pulled a handkerchief from his pocket, and wiped his brow. "I feel ill."

When one of the officers went straight to April, Lin hurried to Anton. "Are you woozy? Do you need to sit down?"

"No, I'm fine. I'm relieved and thankful. When I heard that gunshot, I almost passed out." The older man looked at Lin. "Do you know how angry Libby would have been with me if anything had happened to you?" He smiled, and Lin chuckled.

Leonard and Nicky walked over to their partners. Lin picked up the dog, and then they all reached out their arms to embrace each other in a three person and one dog group hug.

28

A week later, Viv and John hosted a cookout in their backyard to celebrate the apprehension of the Mailman and that everyone had come out of it safe and sound. Lin was sitting at the deck table with Libby and Anton.

"You bet I would have been furious with you if anything happened to Carolin," Libby told Anton. "She is a healer and a helper and we have to do all we can to protect her."

Anton glanced at Lin. "See, I told you she'd be angry with me."

"You can't blame Anton for things like that. I entered that apartment to keep April from harm. I entered freely, and without reservation. I knew there were risks."

"You can't put yourself in danger," Libby clucked.

"I couldn't just stand there and let April die."

"In the future, just call the police and tell them you think someone might have a weapon and someone is in danger. Then let them handle it." Libby looked down at the dog sitting with Queenie on one of the lounge chairs. "The real hero is Nicky. He is selfless, intelligent, and quick-thinking. Thank you, fine animal."

Nicky wagged his tail and looked almost like he was smiling.

"Come down here and play some games with us," Viv called.

Lin and Anton joined Viv, April, Jim and Leah Blake, Heather and Leonard in a game of badminton while Libby, Jeff, John, Kurt, and his wife competed in a game of cornhole.

When the playing was over for a while, Jeff and John went to get the grill started and everyone else gathered around the drinks table.

Jim had his arm around April's shoulders as he sipped from his glass. "I don't want to let go of her."

April smiled. "It's nice not to have to worry anymore."

"Are you up for telling us what happened that

night?" Heather asked. "If not, that's perfectly all right."

"I'm happy to talk about it." April nodded. "Eileen came up to me on the street in front of my apartment. She chatted and then asked if she could come inside. She had some things she wanted to order from my basket business. I fell for it, and once inside, she turned into a monster. She pulled out the gun, then bound my arms and gagged me. She planned to take me to her car. I decided right then and there, that I was not getting in that car. She could shoot me in the street, but I was going to kick and fight like heck and I wasn't getting into the car. After she bound my arms, I dropped to the floor and wouldn't budge."

"You sure were brave," Viv told the young woman.

"I wanted to live and I knew if I got into her car, Eileen would kill me. I would fight her to stay alive."

Leah hugged her daughter and brushed away some tears.

"But I didn't have to because the cavalry came to help me," April beamed. "Thank you," she told Lin, Leonard, Anton, and Nicky. "From the bottom of my heart."

April and Leah went inside the house to get some appetizers they'd brought along.

While others were talking or helping with the food, Jim said to Lin, "We've heard from the police that Eileen wanted to hurt our family because Leah hurt her relationship with Michael by having an affair with him. She couldn't let go of her rage so she started her campaign of harassment. Her hate and resentment grew over the years and she decided that now was the time to really make us pay. She decided to kill April." The last words caught in his throat.

"It's too bad she didn't seek help for her anger and sadness over what had happened," Lin shook her head. "So much misery would have been avoided. I'm so glad this whole thing can be put behind you now."

"Thanks to all of you. We're very grateful."

"Will you be staying on-island? Have you left behind the idea to move away?" Lin asked.

"We're absolutely staying." Jim had a wide grin on his face.

"I'm happy to hear that."

"Did you know Michael is filing for divorce and will be selling the Main Street house?"

"I'm not surprised he'll be ending his marriage,

but I didn't know the house went up for sale. I don't think Jeff and Kurt know about that either."

"Michael intends to have the restoration finished before listing the house. He knows the work that's being done will contribute to a higher price for the place."

"That makes sense. Jeff and Kurt will be pleased to hear their work will be able to continue."

With the sun setting, John went around the yard and lit the lanterns and the torches that were placed at the edges of the garden. The deck and patio lights twinkled overhead and when the food was ready, everyone took seats at the long table on the patio.

The meal was delicious and the warm feelings of friendship were even better. After eating, John and Viv brought out their guitars and for another hour, everyone sang along to the music. A few people even got up and danced.

When the gathering was over, Lin, Jeff, Viv, and John sat on the deck with coffees.

"That was great," Jeff said. "Everyone had a good time."

"We're lucky to have so many nice people in our lives," Viv smiled.

Lin told them that Michael Salem was going to sell the Main Street house, but assured Jeff that he wouldn't list the place until the work was done. She looked over at John. "Why don't you approach Michael? I don't think he has an agent yet to handle the sale."

"You're reading my mind." John laughed. "As soon as you said he was selling, I decided I'd try to talk to him tomorrow."

"Nothing slips by my husband," Viv chuckled. "Especially when it comes to money." She leaned back in her chair and sighed. "There were actually two secrets to solve this time. The secret that Adam was killed and thrown into the inner harbor, and the one hiding Eileen's murderous intentions. I'll just never understand how people can do such horrible things to each other."

"Adam was murdered when he was a young man. He tried to warn us that April was in danger. He didn't want her to lose her life like he had lost his." Lin looked up at the twinkling stars. "I'd like to go see our ghost."

"Now?" Jeff asked her.

"Yeah. I went the other day, but Kurt and some of the workers arrived so I had to leave. I need to go see him."

"Okay. We can stop there on the way home," Jeff suggested.

"You have the key with you?" Jeff asked his wife.

Lin nodded and opened the door, and she, Jeff, and Nicky went up to the second floor. She looked at the desk in the corner.

"Adam? It's Lin. I want to talk to you." She waited and after a few minutes, she noticed some shimmering particles by the desk.

She told him all about what happened with April, how Eileen had been arrested, and that April was safe and unharmed.

"I didn't understand that you were upset when Eileen came into the house because you knew she was the Mailman and was planning to kill April. I didn't link your upset to her. Eventually, I thought that Michael might be the perpetrator. I missed your signals and I'm sorry about that."

The shimmering particles seemed to grow brighter.

"Our friend Anton also discovered a letter that Lilibeth wrote to her sister. At the time, Lilibeth was in her sixties and her health was poor. She wrote and told her sister what happened to you. George and his brother killed you right here in this house and then dropped your body into the inner harbor. That's why

I felt you when I was on the Linton-Campbell's dock. I sensed your body sinking under the water." She brushed at her eyes. "I'm sorry you didn't get to live your life. I'm sorry your time was stolen from you."

Jeff stepped forward and quietly took Lin's hand.

"Do you know that Lilibeth never married?" Lin went on talking to the ghost. "She didn't. She couldn't let go of her love for you. She wrote in her letter to her sister that she hoped to reunite with you once she passed."

The particles by the desk sparkled.

"Did you look for Lilibeth? Do you know how to find her?" Lin and Jeff walked closer to the desk. "Do you want my help?"

The piece of paper appeared on the desk and the pen floated on the air. In a moment, the pen fell to the paper and moved over it forming words.

Lin leaned to see what was written.

Yes My Lilibeth Yes Yes

"I'm going to close my eyes. I'll try to locate her. You can help me. Think about her. Picture her in your mind. Feel her in your heart. Remember the love you shared."

Lin turned to face Jeff and she took his other hand in hers and then closed her eyes. She concentrated on the love she felt for Jeff and the love she felt from him. She allowed her mind to clear and let the love in her heart float into the universe.

Lilibeth. Adam is waiting for you. He's here. He's always been here. Waiting for you.

Lin saw a flash in her head that was so bright it startled her and her eyes popped open and she stepped back.

Jeff touched her cheek. "I'm here. You're okay."

Nicky rubbed his head on her leg.

Lin stepped closer, wrapped her arms around Jeff, and lay her cheek against his chest. She was so, so tired.

When Nicky woofed, Lin smiled and reached down to pet her sweet dog. When she stood up, something caught her eye through the window.

She gasped.

On the lawn in front of the house stood two shimmering figures ... a young man and a young woman, their hands locked together. They looked up at the window and smiled.

Lin pressed her hand against the glass as tears flowed from her eyes.

Lilibeth. Adam. You found one another.

The atoms that made up the spirits flared and

sparked with gold and silver light, and in a moment, they were gone.

"Was something out there?" Jeff put his hand on Lin's shoulder.

"Lilibeth and Adam. They're together again," Lin whispered as she put her arm around Jeff's waist.

After looking out the window for a few moments, Jeff asked, "Shall we go home?"

Lin glanced to the desk. The pen and paper were gone.

"Yes." She touched her husband's cheek and traced her finger along his jawline before leaning in and kissing him. "Let's go home."

Lin smiled at the dog. "What do you say, Nick?"

The dog woofed and trotted happily out of the room with Lin and Jeff following after.

THANK YOU FOR READING!

Books by J.A. Whiting can be found here:
www.amazon.com/author/jawhiting

To hear about new books and book sales, please sign
up for our mailing list at:
www.jawhiting.com

Your email will never be sold, shared, or spammed.

If you enjoyed the book, please consider leaving a
review. A few words are all that's needed. It would be
very much appreciated.

BOOKS BY J. A. WHITING

OLIVIA MILLER MYSTERIES (not cozy)

SWEET COVE PARANORMAL COZY MYSTERIES

LIN COFFIN PARANORMAL COZY MYSTERIES

CLAIRE ROLLINS COZY MYSTERIES

PAXTON PARK PARANORMAL COZY MYSTERIES

SEEING COLORS PARANORMAL COZY MYSTERIES

ELLA DANIELS WITCH COZY MYSTERIES

COZY BOX SETS

SWEET ROMANCES by JENA WINTER

BOOKS BY J.A. WHITING & ARIEL SLICK

GOOD HARBOR WITCHES PARANORMAL COZY MYSTERIES

BOOKS BY J.A. WHITING & AMANDA DIAMOND

PEACHTREE POINT COZY MYSTERIES

DIGGING UP SECRETS PARANORMAL COZY MYSTERIES

BOOKS BY J.A. WHITING & NELL MCCARTHY

HOPE HERRING PARANORMAL COZY MYSTERIES

TIPPERARY CARRIAGE COMPANY COZY MYSTERIES

VISIT US

www.jawhiting.com

www.bookbub.com/authors/j-a-whiting

www.amazon.com/author/jawhiting

www.facebook.com/jawhitingauthor

www.bingebooks.com/author/ja-whiting

J. A. WHITING BOOKS

Printed in Great Britain
by Amazon

42075867R00172